Burmese Monk's Tales

COLLECTED, TRANSLATED, AND INTRODUCED BY

Maung Htin Aung

PARIYATTI PRESS
an imprint of
Pariyatti Publishing
www.pariyatti.org

ISBN: 978-1-68172-327-3 (Print)

ISBN: 978-1-68172-049-4 (PDF)

ISBN: 978-1-93875-440-1 (ePub)

ISBN: 978-1-93875-441-8 (Mobi)

Library of Congress Control Number: 2016909916

First Pariyatti Edition, 2016

Maung Htin Aung was a Visiting Professor at Wake Forest College, 1965–66. He was the Rector of the University of Rangoon from 1946 to 1958, and the Vice-Chancellor in 1959. He was the author of Burmese Drama (1937), Burmese Folk-Tales (1948), Burmese Law Tales (1962), Folk Elements in Burmese Buddhism (1962), and The Stricken Peacock: An Account of Anglo-Burmese Relations 1752–1948 (1965).

Design on title page: an excerpt from The Pageant of King Mindon (1865). Royal palanquin derived by Warren Infield from a contemporary document reproduced in Memoirs of the Archaeological Survey of India (1925).

Acknowledgments

My grateful thanks are due to the Venerable Aggamahāpaṇḍita Thiri Sayadaw, head of the Thiri Mingalaryone Monastery, Kemmendine, Rangoon, and a member of the Council of Ten Great Abbots of the Dwarya sect, for his guidance and advice in my study of the history of Buddhism in Burma.

My grateful thanks are also due to Professor U E. Maung, M.A., Emeritus Professor of Burmese in the University of Rangoon, and his wife (my elder sister) Daw Mya Mu, M.A., formerly Reader in Burmese at the same University, for their guidance and help.

I also take this opportunity to express my appreciation of the following former pupils of mine who assisted me in the compilation of this work: U Ohn Gaing, B.A., B.L., C.A., of the Port of Rangoon, and U Ba Thein, BA., B.L., of the Burma Audit and Accounts Service.

This is the second of two books which I was able to complete as a scholar-in-residence at Columbia University in the School of International Affairs during the academic year 1963–64, and for that privilege and opportunity I am grateful to President Grayson Kirk and Dean Andrew W. Cordier.

MAUNG HTIN AUNG

Uris Hall
Columbia University in the
City of New York
June 30, 1965

Table of Contents

Introduction

Burmese Buddhism
on the Eve of British Conquest

he Monk's Tales contained in this collection were first told during that dark decade of Burmese history (1876–85), when the coming event of the British conquest of the whole country was perturbing the Burmese people. For the first time since the eleventh century the future of Burmese Buddhism became uncertain, and there was widespread fear, both in Upper Burma still under a Burmese king and in Lower Burma already under British rule, that the final fall of the Burmese kingdom would result in the total extinction of both the national religion and the Burmese way of life. Told with the purpose of allaying this anxiety and fear, these tales give a full and faithful résumé and appraisal of the position of Burmese Buddhism on the eve of the British conquest of 1886.

THE CLERGY AND THE PEOPLE. As the background of the tales is the close and intimate relationship that existed between the clergy and the laity, it is necessary to realize the unique position enjoyed by the Buddhist clergy in Burmese society. Although it may sound paradoxical at first, it is correct to say that the clergy was both outside and inside the society. A Buddhist monk, donning the yellow robe and taking the higher ordination, discarded his former life, profession, property, and family, and became free of the shackles of the mundane world. Under Burmese law, from the moment he took the higher ordination, his marriage automatically was dissolved; his ties to his family were cut, and he lost all property and civil rights. Thus he became an entire outsider to society. However, since the days of King Anawrahta (1044–77), Burmese monks had been the teachers of the laity, not only in religious learning but also in secular learning. The first monks sent to the outlying parts of the kingdom by King Anawrahta and his primate Shin Arahan convened the people to the new faith, not only by preaching to them the essentials of Buddhism, but also by teaching them how to read and write. Even up to the present day, the only Burmese word for "school" is *kyaung*, which means "monastery." Following the tradition started in Anawrahta's time, the monks remained the educators of the people, both young and old, until 1886. When a boy attained the age of five or six years he was sent to the nearest monastery to wait on the elder monks, to go with them on their morning rounds of begging for alms, and to study reading, writing, and arithmetic in the afternoon. He had his fun like all children in the late afternoon when he romped and played in the garden attached to the monastery. But he had to conform to the general monastic discipline of the institution, and thus he grew up under the watchful eyes of the abbot. When he attained the age of fifteen years it became necessary for him to go through an initiation ceremony, put on the yellow robe, and take the lower ordination. As he had to keep only certain vows, which were not very different from the Ten Precepts which ordinary laymen kept on Sabbath days, he did not find his new life too irksome. He could leave the monastery at his own choice after a period of four months to one year, and ordinarily he would do so, to be received back into lay society as an educated and trained adult. Now he could look for work, and in due course choose a bride for himself. If he was a little more ambitious, he would go to a master craftsman and apprentice himself for three years, hoping to become a journeyman at the end of the period. If he was a more brilliant student, he might stay on as a novice until he reached the minimum age for the higher ordination, namely twenty years, studying, in addition to the scriptures, the "legitimate" subjects of literature, history, and law. Although the *Vinaya* rules prohibited monks from practicing medicine, alchemy, and astrology, Burmese monks had always been interested in these subjects as scholars, and doubtless the young novice would be instructed in these subjects also at the monastery. When he attained the age of twenty years he could still leave the monastery and be selected as a civil servant either by the king or by his representative, or given a clerkship by an advocate, or be chosen as an assistant by a physician. If he should be exceptionally religious, however, he would take the higher ordination and remain in the monastery or go to the great monastic colleges at the king's capital for further studies in the scriptures. Even if he had left the order at the age of sixteen, or of twenty, he would find time to come to the monastery and get advice and instruction from his former teachers. According to a Burmese-Buddhist belief, there were Five Great "Beings" to be constantly remembered, honored, and worshiped, namely, the Buddha, His Teachings, the Monk, the Teacher, and the Parent. Thus the monks were worshiped and esteemed not only as monks but also as teachers. The most respectful term of address in the Burmese language, namely, "my lord," was applicable only to the Buddha, the king or his senior representatives, the monks, and one's own parents. Burmese society had always been "classless" in that a person's position in society was determined not by his birth but by his talent and ability. Wealth was more or less evenly distributed, and there were very few really rich or really poor people. The majority were peasant proprietors. A person on attaining the legal age of maturity, whether male or female, acquired full rights of property and inheritance. The king himself, in theory at least, was just an adult who had been elected to his high office. There never was a hereditary nobility, and the officials appointed by the king automatically lost office with the latter's death or dethronement. Thus the monks were the only elite in a society of equal individuals. The abbot of the village monastery was a well-respected figure, not only in his own village but in the neighboring villages also, for he had spent ten years as a fully ordained monk and some more years as a senior monk before his installation as an abbot, and during that long period of time he had taught many generations of village boys and girls, and had visited and preached in the villages nearby. His advice was sought in their more difficult domestic problems by the villagers and in their more difficult administrative problems by the king's officials. Although he kept himself aloof from the normal domestic life of a villager, he would scold an ungrateful son or an unjust father, just as, although ordinarily above politics and official matters, he would chide a royal representative for an unjust administrative matter, and would even demand the life and liberty of a convicted criminal if there was an obvious miscarriage of justice. There were instances of an abbot's acting as the emissary for peace between factions warring for a throne, or between kingdoms fighting for supremacy. When the abbot died, his passing away was mourned by all the villagers nearby. His body, embalmed in honey, lay in state, and when the harvest was over it was cremated with great pomp and ceremony.

THE MONASTERY. Before 1852 every village had its own monastery. Even a hamlet had at least a one-room structure with a single monk in residence. A larger village or town had more than one monastery. In the larger towns like Pegu, Prome, Toungoo, Amarapura, Ava, and Shwebo, which had been capitals in earlier reigns, and in the golden city of Mandalay, there were large monasteries which were really monastic colleges with the abbots and the senior monks acting as tutors to hundreds of junior monks in residence. The average-sized monastery in a town or village had an abbot, two or three monks who had spent at least ten years as members of the order and who were thus known as senior monks, and five or six junior monks. In addition, there was a fluctuating number of novices and boys studying in the monastery. As the monks were prohibited by their vows from handling gold or silver or money, there was a lay brother who served the monastery as its steward. He also acted as cook and prepared the evening meals for the boys in residence, and occasionally the morning meals for the monks themselves, when a housewife, too busy to cook herself, brought to him rice, raw meat, fish, and vegetables and requested him to prepare and offer them to the monks on her behalf.

Except on grounds of illness or infirmity, it was obligatory for every monk and novice to go round the village in the morning with their begging bowls to receive alms food. The food received was pooled and eaten together on their return to their monastery. However, they could accept an invitation by a villager to come and take the morning meal at his house. Such invitations were usually made on Sabbath days, namely, the eighth day of the waxing moon, the full-moon day, the eighth day of the waning moon, and the day of no moon. And invitations were also given on days which were of importance to the particular villager, as, for example, the anniversaries of his parents' deaths, or the birthday of his wife, his child, or himself. On Sabbath days, many Sabbath-keepers came to the monastery with offerings of alms food for the monks.

A monastery consisted of more than one building. In addition to the buildings occupied by the monks, the novices, and the boys, there were an ordination hall, a preaching hall where the abbot or a senior monk preached to the congregation on Sabbath days, and one or two rest-houses for the Sabbath-keepers. The monastery usually stood in a large garden of fruit and flower trees.

MONASTIC DISCIPLINE. The monastery was a place of decorum and discipline, and monastic life was austere. The boys were required to keep the Five Precepts; the novices, their ninety-five rules of training; and the monks, two hundred and twenty-seven rules. The monks were exhorted to meditate, and all were required to be diligent in study. Only the lay brother was not under any special rule of discipline, but he also kept the Eight Precepts on many days and occasionally the Ten Precepts. The monks and novices wore yellow robes and the lay brother usually dressed in white, but the boys wore ordinary dress. The monks, novices, and lay brothers had shaven heads, but the boys wore their hair long until the day of their initiation ceremony. The work of keeping the monastery and its grounds clean was in the hands of the junior monks, the novices, and the boys. Whereas the boys were under the general charge of the monks, every novice was under a preceptor chosen from among the senior monks. Punishment for breach of discipline on the part of the boys was in the form of extra labor in keeping the monastery clean, unless the case was a serious one, when the punishment would be caning by the abbot. The ninety-five rules of conduct which novices had to follow were divided into three groups: ten rules of "distinction," ten rules of "punishment," and seventy- five rules of "decorum." The breach of any rule in the first group by a novice was deemed to result in a loss of his "distinction" or "identity" as a novice, and he was accordingly unfrocked and expelled from the monastery. Punishment for a breach of a rule in the second group was exhortation for better conduct by the abbot, together with extra hours of manual labor. The breach of one of the seventy-five rules of decorum merely brought on the culprit's head words of reproach from his preceptor.

The day for the inmates of the monastery began at dawn when their reveille was sounded by the lay brother beating on a hollow log with a stick. The monks, the novices, and the boys, after ablutions and prayers, assembled in the refectory for a cup of rice gruel, which the lay brother had prepared. The boys then swept and cleaned, while the monks prepared to go out. At about seven o'clock the monks and the novices, attended by the boys, went round the village with their begging bowls, returning at about ten o'clock. They took their meal at about eleven o'clock, and by noon all the begging bowls had been cleaned. After an hour of rest all assembled for their studies and lessons until an hour before sundown. Then the novices and some of the boys again swept and cleaned the premises while other boys romped about. When darkness had fallen the boys took their evening meal, and afterwards all the inmates of the monastery assembled for evening worship. The novices and the boys studied their lessons for about an hour, and at about eight o'clock they went to bed. The monks meditated or assembled to discuss and debate a knotty problem of the monastery or a particular matter of monastic discipline or some special topic from the scriptures. By about ten o'clock, the monks retired except for one or two who would continue meditation far into the night. In addition to their daily routine the monks from all the monasteries in one parish had to hold an assembly on every full-moon day and no-moon day, to repeat and recite together the 227 Vinaya Rules. Such an assembly often constituted a confessional. Of the 227 rules, four were known as "rules of defeat." The breach of one of the four by a monk amounted to a "defeat" for him as a monk, and automatically he ceased to be one. Of the remaining rules, thirteen were grouped together because the breach of any one of them required a confession by the offender before an assembly of monks. The remaining rules, which included the seventy-five rules of decorum binding on a novice, were listed together in groups according to differing degrees of seriousness, but absolution for the breach of any one of them was obtainable by a confession to another monk. The monks often left their monasteries to go on a pilgrimage, to visit other monasteries, or to stay in a forest hermitage, but they were forbidden to travel or change residence during the three months of lent, which coincided with the rainy season in a monsoon land. During these three months the monks took up permanent residence in a particular monastery "to keep the lent," and a monk's seniority was counted in monastic parlance by the lents he had kept instead of by years. For example, an abbot's age and seniority would be described as fifty years of age and thirty kept lents.

In spite of the austere way of life and the strict code of discipline, it would be wrong to think that a Burmese monastery was a gloomy and an awesome place. On the contrary, it was fair and pleasant. The monks retained the optimistic outlook and the sense of humor characteristic of the Burmese people. The lay brother usually was a droll fellow whose eccentricities amused everyone who came in contact with him. The boys, notwithstanding an occasional caning by the abbot, remained mischievous as ever; according to a folk belief, demons and evil spirits were more afraid of the catapult of the monastery boys than of the scriptural recitations of the pious abbot. The belles of the village often threw loving glances at the novices, for the time would soon come when many of them would be leaving the monastery to become eligible young bachelors. On Sabbath days the villagers, young and old, male and female, matron and maid, would come to the monastery with their gifts of alms food, the novices would join in the throng, and the monastery boys, free for the day from the burden of their lessons, would be reunited with their parents, would eat like little kings, and would frolic and play all over the place.

THE LAITY AND THEIR BUDDHISM. Most European writers on Burmese Buddhism put forward the view that the average Burmese, finding Buddhism too intellectual and too pessimistic, retained their primitive animistic beliefs, merely covering them with a veneer of Buddhism. Although it is true that originally many of the pre-Buddhist cults struggled for survival by giving lip service to Buddhism, as time passed, the cults themselves disappeared, leaving only those beliefs and practices which were acceptable to Buddhism. Admittedly Burmese Buddhism was not a single canonical religion, but it had a uniformity and a unity which made it the national religion of the various racial groups found living in Burma. The more discerning among Western scholars noticed this, and thus R. H. Slater wrote: "It is nearer the truth to say that (the Burman) has added to his Buddhism just so much animism as suits his Buddhism."

From the very beginning of its history, Buddhism was divided into Buddhism for the ascetic and Buddhism for the layman, or, to use academic phraseology, "advanced" Buddhism and "elements" of Buddhism. The path of purity along which Buddhists traveled towards Nirvana had to be traveled in stages. For the ascetic and the spiritually advanced, Buddhism pointed out the advantages and the desirability of renouncing the world, and exhorted them to lead a life of continence and abstinence and to work out their own salvation by means of meditation. On the other hand, for those who had yet to achieve spiritual maturity, Buddhism explained that a layman could obtain true happiness and tranquillity by fulfilling his domestic and social duties and by the practice of loving-kindness, charity, and morality. Buddhist monks were never priests, and as Buddhism considered ritual to be of no importance at all, the intercession of the clergy between the laity and their religion was never necessary. In observing the Five Precepts or the Eight Precepts, the layman was not obeying any orders from a superior, but merely honoring his own undertaking to refrain from doing certain acts. There was no real need for a layman to "take" the Five Precepts from a monk or for a monk to "give" him the Five Precepts. Nonetheless, because of a natural human desire for some ritual in the practice of their religion, and as an expression of their great respect for the clergy, the laity evolved the custom of taking the Precepts from a monk. In actual fact, the monk merely recited the formula of the Precepts and the congregation repeated it after him. But every layman realized that the custom was not essential to his keeping of the Precepts, and therefore whenever it was not possible for him to go before a monk, he would recite the formula on his own.

The Burmese layman always turned to the monks on all occasions of domestic joy or sorrow, and would make offering of alms food and other necessities to them. Even without the excuse of a special occasion, the layman would make the offering just to show his respect for the religion and with a desire to gain merit. Three occasions were specially associated with the offering of alms: moving into a house for the first time, holding an initiation or ear-boring ceremony, and a death in the household. A marriage in Burmese law and custom constituted only a civil contract between two competent parties, the bride and the bridegroom, and therefore it was entirely outside the sphere of religion. However, when the newly married couple moved into a house of their own, they would mark the occasion with offering of alms. The initiation ceremony of a boy constituted a religious occasion, for after the usual festivities the boy would take the lower ordination. A young girl, on attaining puberty, went through an equivalent ceremony, the ear-boring ceremony. When a member of a household had died, monks were invited to the house the same day or, if the death had taken place after the hour of noon, the following morning, and offered alms food. At the funeral a further offering of robes and other necessities was made. On all occasions, after the offerings, the most senior monk present gave the formula of the Praise of the Buddha, which the congregation repeated three times; then he gave the formula of Taking Refuge in the Buddha, in his Teachings, and in the Order, which the congregation also repeated three times; finally he gave the formula of the Five Precepts (Eight Precepts on Sabbath days). The full-moon days, marking the beginning of lent, the end of lent, and the completion of one month after the end of lent were considered by the laity to be very important days in the monastic calendar, and accordingly special offerings of alms food and other necessities were made. On the full-moon day which occurred one month after the end of lent, at every monastery a great ceremony was held in which robes were offered to every monk present.

The Burmese had always been fond of music, dancing, strolling players, and puppet shows. Even though the Eight Precepts of the Sabbath days included a rule of training to refrain from participating in, watching, or listening to any musical or theatrical performance, they did not consider any celebration or ceremony complete without some music, dancing, and a show. This resulted in a gay and festive air, which pervaded the whole village, especially on the day of an initiation ceremony, and the full-moon day marking the end of lent.

THE CLERGY AND THE KING. The king himself, notwithstanding his pomp and power, was just a layman who had received his education from the monks and who had spent a period of time as a novice in a monastery. He was, however, the chief patron of the religion and as such possessed the royal prerogative of appointing the primate. The primate was responsible for the maintenance of order and discipline in the ranks of the clergy; accordingly he was under a duty to take necessary disciplinary measures against wayward members of the order, and he heard, decided, and settled all cases of dispute. He had an ecclesiastical council to assist him. Dividing the whole kingdom into a number of ecclesiastical districts, for each district he appointed a local abbot as his representative. Attached to his office were two lay officials whose duties were to execute his orders and decisions. These officers were the ecclesiastical censor and the commissioner for ecclesiastical lands. Both were royal officials, directly appointed by the king. The ecclesiastical censor maintained a register of monks; although the primate alone could unfrock a wayward monk, the ecclesiastical censor on his own could produce the same effect by scratching out the name of the offender from his register.

Buddhist monks had nowhere ever claimed that they were outside the authority and the laws of the state, but in Burma, because of the special regard and respect paid to the monks, it would have been embarrassing and awkward for both the king and the clergy if a monk were to be arrested and tried as a common criminal. So to prevent such an incident from ever taking place, custom and convention required the ecclesiastical censor to scratch out from his register the name of a monk the moment the latter was accused of a serious crime, with the result that he took his arrest and trial as an ordinary layman and not as a monk. In practice, even that action on the part of the censor was unnecessary, because the primate or his local representative would disrobe a monk when he was accused by the king's officers of a crime. Under Burmese customary law the clergy had the right of giving sanctuary to criminals in that every monk could ask for the life and freedom of any person accused or even convicted of a crime. This right acted against the possibility of abuse of power by the ecclesiastical censor or by any royal official or, for that matter, by the king himself. On the other hand, the monks saw to it that their right of giving sanctuary did not unduly interfere with the royal administration of justice, exercising the right only when there was a grave miscarriage of justice.

In spite of these checks and balances working between the king and the clergy, the clergy never questioned the fact that the king was not only the chief patron of Buddhism and defender of the faith but also the final authority in all ecclesiastical affairs, always remembering that, although Buddhism in its pristine purity never needed the aid of the secular arm, it was Asoka's patronage of Buddhist monks which spread the ancient faith all over Asia, and it was Anawrahta's might that had first made Buddhism the official and national religion of Burma.

Buddhism had never in any place been a single canonical religion, and Burmese Buddhism was no exception. Buddhism encouraged every monk to discuss and to debate any point of doctrine or monastic usage, and only when the discussions resulted in serious controversy did it become necessary for the whole congregation of monks to vote and to express the view of the majority. Even at that point, the minority could leave the congregation and form a group of their own. Thus new schisms could develop and new sects could appear from time to time. Usually the controversy was over the correct interpretation of the particular *Vinaya* rules regarding the ordination and personal conduct of Buddhist monks. Since the *Vinaya* rules were assumed to have crystallized with the death of the Buddha, there could be no question of adding new rules, and therefore the controversy was usually over the interpretation of a particular existing rule. As long as the controversy did not affect the prestige or discipline of the clergy as a whole, neither the primate nor the king would interfere. Thus, after the establishment of a single unified sect in the eleventh century, there had been schisms and sects, but when the First Anglo-Burmese War broke out in 1824, only one sect existed in the whole kingdom.

DECAY OF BUDDHISM IN LOWER BURMA. The First Anglo-Burmese War did not affect Burmese Buddhism very much, and the monks living in the maritime provinces of Arakan and Tenasserim, which had been ceded to the British after the defeat of 1826, were not disheartened as they continued to receive instructions from the primate at the king's capital. In contrast, the Second Anglo-Burmese War (1852), resulting in the conquest of the whole region of Lower Burma by the British, had disastrous consequences for the religion. The monks were distressed at the thought of living under an alien government, and the laity feared that the national religion would be suppressed and persecuted. Mass migrations of monks, both Burmese and Mon, to Upper Burma and rebellions against the new government by both Burmese and Mon resulted. Many towns and villages in Lower Burma came to be without any resident monk, and monasteries fell to neglect and decay. The few monks who remained felt abandoned and lost, and some of them became lax and corrupt. In despair the laity in Lower Burma petitioned the British governor to extend patronage to Buddhism, and appoint a primate so as to enforce discipline and order among the ranks of the clergy remaining in Lower Burma, but he refused to do so. Queen Victoria in her famous proclamation as the empress of India had promised religious toleration to her conquered subjects; following the letter rather than the spirit of the proclamation, the British government in Lower Burma kept itself aloof from the religious affairs of the Burmese people who were under its rule. But conditions in Burma were entirely different from those prevailing in India. In India since the eleventh century, which had ushered in the Muslim conquest of the subcontinent, there had been a continual struggle and conflict between the two religions, Hinduism and Islam. In contrast, since the same century, Buddhism had been the official, national, and popular religion of the Burmese.

In the circumstances, the refusal of the British government to extend patronage to Buddhism was not only misunderstood but also resented. The position was made even worse by the following facts. First, the Christian missionaries at Rangoon even before the Second Anglo-Burmese war openly showed contempt for Burmese national and religious institutions, and sided with the British when that war broke out. After Rangoon had fallen and British rule was extended to cover all Lower Burma, these missionaries identified themselves with the conquerors and gleefully shared their triumph. Second, when the Church of England was established in Lower Burma for the benefit of the English soldiers and officials, its clergymen were naturally paid officials of the government. The Burmese could not understand why the British government should grant patronage to its own Christian religion and not to the Buddhist religion of the Burmese also.

KING MINDON. King Mindon, who ascended the Burmese throne in 1852 after Pegu had been lost, was one of the ablest monarchs in Burmese history, and he persevered to maintain the independence of his small kingdom. With all the seaports in British hands, the Burmese kingdom lay at their mercy, and Mindon fully realized the necessity of coming to terms with the enemy. The most devout of Burmese kings, Mindon considered it his bounden duty to take measures which would preserve Burmese Buddhism in all its glory for many generations to come even if Burmese kings should reign no more. The position of the religion in Lower Burma caused him great anxiety, and he felt that, as a vacuum had been created by the British refusal to extend patronage to Buddhism, it was his responsibility to sustain the religion in that region, although it was no longer part of his territory. Realizing that measures to purify and preserve the national religion must first be taken in his own kingdom, he was in constant consultation not only with the primate and the ecclesiastical council, but also with many other learned and pious monks to devise ways and means. He planned to re-crown the Shwedagon pagoda at Rangoon with a spire of gold and precious stones, although this great national shrine was in British territory. He planned to hold also a great synod of Buddhist monks, the fifth of its kind in the history of Theravada Buddhism. The importance and the magnitude of this undertaking could be seen from the fact that the third synod had been held by the emperor Asoka himself, and the fourth had taken place in Ceylon as long ago as 88 b.c. King Mindon extended and improved the system of holding public examinations in the scriptures for monks and for the laity. Like King Dhammazedi (1472–92) before him, he purified the clergy by encouraging learning. He also took King Bodawpaya (1782–1819) as an example, and introduced stern measures to suppress and punish breaches of monastic discipline. Above all, he encouraged many monks to return or migrate or at least pay occasional visits to Lower Burma so as to keep the light of Buddhism burning brightly in that region, although under alien rule.

KING MINDON AND HIS CRITICS. Mindon was not a hardened soldier as Bodawpaya was, and he found it difficult to deal ruthlessly with those who dared to disagree with him. Like all reformers, he was criticized by monks and laymen alike, who accused him of either going too far in his reforms or not going far enough. Unlike Bodawpaya, he had to face also the problem of luxurious living on the part of the monks. His very success in reviving interest in religious learning made the people more devout, and as his economic reforms coupled with the extension of overseas commerce through Lower Burma had increased the wealth of his people, they showered the monks with endowments and personal gifts, including such items as velvet robes, silken slippers, and scented soap. Mindon, through his great monks and the ecclesiastical censor, attempted to curb the use of luxury articles by monks, and even went to the extreme of prohibiting the monks from using umbrellas and footwear except in case of sickness. This question of luxurious living on the part of the monks was brought to a head by a lay scholar of great repute, who started a movement to denounce the entire clergy, putting forward the thesis that monks were mere parasites of the great religion. During Bodawpaya's time another lay scholar, disgusted with the controversy over the proper method of wearing robes, had advocated that the clergy be disregarded by laymen, and had been promptly executed by the king. Mindon, after some hesitation, ordered the execution of the offending scholar as a dangerous heretic, amidst protests from both the clergy and the laity. Some monks, although pious themselves, resented the intrusion of the ecclesiastical censor and his inspectors into their monasteries and felt that the ecclesiastical council was surrendering the independence of the clergy to the secular arm. King Mindon was also criticized for his extensive conferment of the title of *Sayadaw* or "royal teacher." Originally this title was reserved for the monk who was the actual tutor of the king, or who had been the king's tutor when he was still a prince, but in the course of centuries the title came to be conferred on those monks who were regularly consulted by the king on matters pertaining to the religion. The reign of Mindon was especially rich in great monks of immense learning, and the king honored them all as royal teachers. This made the title cheap and prompted the people in Lower Burma to apply it to some of their own monks, without the king's sanction.

The most bitter critic of Mindon and his ecclesiastical council was the Bhamo Sayadaw, himself one of those great monks often consulted by the king. A scholar of great learning, he possessed a caustic wit and a bitter tongue. He challenged the authority of the ecclesiastical censor to visit his monastery, and made fun of the king's edicts in ballads and lyrics. He was a master of the epigram, and his wit amused his listeners and annoyed the king. Although he was above any suspicion of luxurious living because of his known austerity, he was especially bitter against the edict prohibiting the use of umbrellas and footwear. Finally he wrote bitter lampoons against not only the ecclesiastical council but also the king's Privy Council, and this insult to the authority and good name of the two supreme administrative bodies was so great that the king was constrained to exile the monk to his native town of Bhamo. Sometime later, on the petition of the queen, Mindon relented and sent a royal party to conduct him back in full honor to Mandalay. The monk came down in the royal boat, but when it reached Sagaing on the opposite bank of Mandalay, he suddenly decided to make his permanent residence there and disembarked, sending to the king the sarcastic excuse that, as a convicted criminal, he should not contaminate the royal palace by his presence. This refusal of the Bhamo Sayadaw to return to the capital greatly distressed the king.

MIGRATIONS TO THE SAGAING HILLS. As a corollary to the accusation of luxurious living, there was a revival of the ancient controversy as to whether the forest or the monastery was the ideal habitat for a Buddhist monk. This controversy went back even to the lifetime of the Buddha. One of the impossible demands made by Devadutta to the Buddha so as to create a schism in the ranks of the clergy was that monks should be required to dwell in the forest instead of in monasteries near towns and villages. Buddha himself had been a wandering ascetic, and Arahat Kassapa, ranked next only to Arahats Sariputara and Mogghallanna, was famous for his austere living; he dwelt in the forest and wore robes made out of shrouds abandoned at the cemetery. But the Buddha declined to promulgate a rule which would cause hardship to the average monk among his following. Some of the great monks on the ecclesiastical council themselves often retired to a forest hermitage for one or two months every year, but naturally the council disapproved of the controversy. Nonetheless, some senior monks migrated to the wooded valleys and natural caves on the hills across the river and near the small town of Sagaing. Their pupils followed, and in the wake of the pupils came enthusiastic, devout, and excited laymen and laywomen. Very soon the hills became dotted with brick monasteries, preaching halls, and rest houses, far more costly than the wooden monasteries of Mandalay. The small town of Sagaing became almost a city, and the Sagaing Hills echoed and re-echoed with the humming sound of prayer and recitation.

CHALLENGE FROM WITHIN: THE NGETTWIN SAYADAW. The single unified sect which emerged after Bodawpaya's strong measures now showed signs of disintegration. Known as the Thudhamma Sect, because it was under the authority of the Thudhamma or ecclesiastical council, it had been without a rival for some eighty years. The challenge to the authority of the ecclesiastical council came from within the inner circle of the king. The tutor of Mindon's chief queen was a pious monk who had written a number of learned treatises on the religion, and the queen had built for him a magnificent monastery. Although himself a great monk often consulted by the king, he took part in the migration of monks from the royal city to the Sagaing hills, and went to reside in a more distant part of the cliffs. The place was so inaccessible and so thickly wooded that it was known as Ngettwin, meaning "the cave of birds" or "the cave of malaria." The Ngettwin Sayadaw boldly preached that prevailing practices in the religion needed radical changes. Insisting that meditation was essential to a Buddhist, and that charity and mere morality, without the right mental attitude and awareness, were not enough, he was of the opinion that the centuries-old practice of offering flowers, candles, food, and water to the images of the Buddha in the pagodas and shrines was not only unnecessary, but also harmful in that the faded flowers and burnt-out candles dirtied a place meant for worship and meditation, and the food constituted an encouragement for rats to come near and dig holes in the foundations of the sacred edifice. He also considered it unnecessary that a monk recite the formula of the Five Precepts for a layman to repeat after him, because unless a person already refrains from killing, stealing, telling untruth, committing adultery, and taking drugs and intoxicants, he is not a Buddhist at all. Moreover, on Sabbath days it was unnecessary for laymen and laywomen to keep all the Eight Precepts, for as lay people they had to lead normal lives; accordingly, he dropped out the precept of not taking food after the hour of noon and the precept of celibacy. But he insisted that every layman and laywoman must practice meditation, especially on the Sabbath.

For the monks, also, he introduced new requirements. In addition to the existing rules of ordination regarding physical, mental, and intellectual fitness, he made it necessary for a person seeking even the lower or preliminary ordination to prove that he had practiced meditation for some time. He required all monks around him to reserve a portion of their day for meditation, emphasizing that meditation was far greater in importance than learning. In addition, he prohibited them from accepting gifts of land or movable property unless the gift was declared to be for monks of all four quarters, meaning that it was intended for the whole clergy and not for a particular monk or a group of monks. Above all, he urged that no monk should reside at a particular place for more than one or two years except for reasons of sickness or debility. He dropped his previous names and titles, assuming the new name of "Ngettwin Sayadaw."

CHALLENGE FROM WITHOUT: the okpo sayadaw. In 1855, when monks from Lower Burma were migrating to Upper Burma, singly and in groups, and many monasteries were falling into neglect and decay, a young abbot from the small town of Okpo, which was halfway between Rangoon and Prome, refused to flee from the British rule and kept the light of monastic learning shining brightly. He heartened his pupils to remain with him and encouraged many monks on their way to Upper Burma via Okpo and Prome to stop and stay at his monastery. His message was that the Buddhist clergy, as long as it followed the rules of *Vinaya* strictly, needed neither protection nor patronage from the secular arm. He gave special emphasis to the study of the *Vinaya* and insisted that only by absolute purity of conduct and behavior could the monks hope to preserve the national religion for their people now under alien rule. As time passed he attracted many monks even from Upper Burma to come and study under him. Although he did not go personally to visit the Ngettwin Sayadaw at Sagaing, some of the latter's ideas seemed to have attracted him. For example, the Ngettwin Sayadaw's insistence that monks should refuse to attend any religious function if there was dancing or music was echoed by the Okpo Sayadaw.

Although he did not accept the thesis that meditation should be required from all, the Okpo Sayadaw agreed that mental attitude was of greater weight than mere action; thus whether a deed was really meritorious or otherwise depended on the mental attitude behind it. Accordingly, he suggested that a change be made in the wording of the following time-honored formula of worship:

I worship the Buddha, His Teachings, and His clergy,
With the action of the body, with the action of the mouth,
And with the action of the thought.

He pointed out that the mere physical act of kneeling and the mere physical act of saying the formula would not by themselves constitute worship, unless there was the right awareness and the right mental attitude. In other words, the mental source of a physical action was of the greatest importance. It followed therefore that a mere offering of alms to a monk without the proper mental attitude was not an act of merit, and a mere intention to offer alms accompanied by the right mental attitude was by itself an act of merit. Similarly, an intention to kill a person, even without the actual deed of killing, was an act of demerit, while the physical act of killing without any intention was not an act of demerit.

The Okpo Sayadaw's suggestion that the formula be changed caused a great controversy among the monks all over the whole country. The finer points of the controversy involved some particular Burmese expressions, Pāli grammar and syntax, and, above all, the conception of liability in Burmese law. A complete explanation cannot be given here. However, it may be mentioned that in Burmese jurisprudence words were considered to be sometimes as important as physical action and trespass could be committed either by action or by word, and that in Burmese law of torts and crimes, contrary to English common law, the question of *mens rea* was of no great importance. The Okpo Sayadaw's critics had no quarrel with the contention that the mental attitude behind an act was the basis for merit or demerit, but they held the view that the established and customary words of worship were quite adequate for the laity at least.

A FRESH CHALLENGE FROM THE OKPO SAYADAW. The Okpo Sayadaw, after repeated study and consideration of the *Vinaya* rules, finally came to the conclusion that the Thudhamma sect had followed only the letter and not the spirit of the particular *Vinaya* rule relating to the holding of the ritual of the higher ordination, first at the ordination hall in a village or town and then in an ordination hall built "over the water." According to the *Vinaya*, a bridge could be built to allay the hardship and trouble monks would have to undergo if they were to swim or wade or take a boat across a stretch of water to the second ordination hall. However, in the course of time, as ordination halls of brick and stone came to be built, a permanent bridge was often constructed to connect the two ordination halls. In many cases, with the passing of time, the water receded or dried up so that the bridge merely passed over a stretch of sandy ground. The Okpo Sayadaw, declaring that the bridge should be only temporary and merely makeshift, and must actually pass over a stretch of water, took again the ceremony of higher ordination for himself, and required all his pupils to do likewise, using a temporary bridge to proceed from the ordination hall on land to the ordination hall "on water." This constituted a very serious challenge to the ecclesiastical council and the Thudhamma sect, and, as by this time many monks had returned to Lower Burma on the suggestion of the king and the council, two rival sects in effect came into being, namely those who had taken the Okpo ordination and those who had taken the Thudhamma ordination. It should, however, be realized that the Okpo Sayadaw never had any intention to rival or challenge the authority of the ecclesiastical council; his sole aim was to purify the clergy in Lower Burma so that it could survive the changes in society which would come in the wake of foreign rule.

AN ATTEMPT AT COMPROMISE: THE SHWEGYIN SAYADAW. A monk from the small town of Shwegyin near Shwebo, which was the first capital of the Alaungpaya dynasty, went down to Lower Burma and studied under the Okpo Sayadaw. On his return to his native town, he was duly installed as an abbot and received from the king the title of "royal tutor." Like his teacher, the Okpo Sayadaw, he maintained that, unless the monks themselves gave up their luxuries and their lax ways, Buddhism in the country would decay, and that corruption among the clergy should be put down by the monks themselves without recourse to the secular arm. He did not question at all the validity of the practices connected with ordination under the ecclesiastical council. He introduced two new rules of conduct in addition to and outside the *Vinaya* rules: after the hour of noon, no betel must be chewed and no tobacco must be taken or smoked. The ecclesiastical council did not consider the Shwegyin Sayadaw to be a rebel against their authority, and the Sayadaw himself started his new movement as a compromise between the extreme puritanic ideas of the Ngettwin and Okpo monks on one hand and the more moderate disciplinary measures of the ecclesiastical council on the other. The followers of the Shwegyin Sayadaw, however, considered themselves as belonging to a sect essentially distinct and different from the established Thudhamma sect. Nonetheless, both the king and the ecclesiastical council continued to extend their patronage to the Shwegyin Sayadaw. In fact, in 1865, when the primate died, King Mindon wanted to appoint the Shwegyin Sayadaw as the new primate; fearing to add to the schism, he refrained from doing so. However, he left the vacancy unfilled. With regard to the Ngettwin Sayadaw, both the king and the ecclesiastical council felt unhappy over his more radical pronouncements, especially his criticism of the offering of flowers and food before the images of the Buddha in pagodas and shrines, but the chief queen continued to regard him as her royal tutor, and he for his part never permitted his followers to regard themselves as forming a separate and different sect until 1887, by which time Mindon was no more and his successor Theebaw had lost his throne.

In 1871 Mindon at long last was able to hold the Great Synod. But by that time the king was a disappointed man, full of forebodings for the future of his kingdom and the welfare of his people. He and the ecclesiastical council concentrated on what they considered to be their main task in the synod: the careful editing and revision of the scriptural texts. A faint attempt at conciliation was made by the synod in placing on record an admission that the formula of worship (criticized by the Okpo Sayadaw) was technically incorrect. The Okpo Sayadaw himself did not attend the synod, and the prejudice against him grew among the clergy of Upper Burma, especially because by this time his followers were referring to him by the title of "Sayadaw" although he had never been consulted and honored by the king. Thus the Great Synod failed to cement together the broken fragments of the Thudhamma sect, for neither the Shwegyin nor the Okpo sect returned to the fold. However, the synod restored to the ecclesiastical council much of its lost prestige and re-established its waning authority all over the country. The holding of the Great Synod also reminded the people of Lower Burma under British rule that Mindon was still the patron of their religion, and it reawakened their feelings of loyalty towards him to such an extent that the British government was constrained to refuse him permission to come and worship in person the great Shwedagon pagoda at Rangoon. This refusal angered the people so much that the British had to allow the king to send an embassy to re-crown the pagoda with a golden spire set with rubies and emeralds. This re-crowning of the Shwedagon pagoda was the climax of King Mindon's work for the preservation of the national religion, and he thought that the position of Buddhism in Upper Burma was now secure. As to its future in Lower Burma, he had his doubts, but he felt that he could do no more. He was now a sick man, and in his dealings with the British he continued to meet disappointment, until the final humiliation came in 1875 when his official contact with the British representative at Mandalay suddenly ceased. The third war between the Burmese kingdom and the British was now inevitable, and its outcome needed no foretelling.

LOWER BURMA IN 1871. The definite decline of the religion in Lower Burma which started in 1852 had been checked, and the vacuum caused in Burmese society by mass migrations of monks had been partially filled by 1871, through the efforts of the Okpo Sayadaw and the return of the monks from Upper Burma on Mindon's appeal. However, in many villages the monasteries remained without any incumbents, and in towns and cities, although their monasteries were again teeming with monks and devotees, Buddhism was assailed by new ideas and new ways of living.

In 1852 the British government, not realizing that monastic schools were a main foundation of Burmese society, allowed them to die and set up lay schools in their place. The Christian missions followed suit by establishing missionary schools. The government schools, in strict conformity with Queen Victoria's proclamation of full religious freedom, refused to give any religious or moral teaching to their pupils, but the mission schools made it compulsory for the pupils to study the Christian Bible. The British government after some ten years discovered that it had made a grave mistake in not preserving the monastic schools, but in trying to make amends, it made the position worse. It introduced the study of Pāli, the classical language of Buddhism and the Burmese people, in the government schools, but the teachers, being Europeans or Indians who had hastily taken up the study of the language, used English textbooks and the Roman alphabet in teaching Pāli, which annoyed or even amused Burmese monks and scholars. In the newly revived monasteries in cities and towns, the government authorized the establishment of new monastic schools, in which the teachers would be monks who had passed a qualifying examination in mathematics and elementary surveying. These new monastic schools were to be under the director of education, as in the case of government schools, and the monk-teachers would be paid monetary stipends. Some monks did open schools in their monasteries under these conditions, but their action was criticized by other monks and by the laymen because it was considered improper that monastic schools should be under the direct control of an official who was a non-Buddhist, and because the *Vinaya* rules did not permit a monk to study nonreligious subjects or to accept money.

Thus the introduction of Pāli into the government school curriculum and the establishment of new monastic schools failed to serve as bridges across the great gulf dividing the new educational system from the old. After contributing further confusion to the chaotic conditions already prevailing in the sphere of religion in Lower Burma, Pāli became merely an easy and optional subject which duller students studied, and the monastic schools died a natural death.

The revival of interest in the religion resulting from the efforts made in that direction by King Mindon and his great monks, and by the Okpo Sayadaw, brought in its wake special problems. Many adults in Lower Burma in their new religious fervor took to a belated and hurried study of the scriptures, without bothering to procure proper guidance from the monks, and, like mushrooms lay preachers appeared in towns and villages. Many of them preached their own ludicrous interpretations of the scriptures and, especially in those villages which had no monks in their monasteries, they succeeded in misleading the people. Some of the lay preachers even expressed themselves in print, and the harm inflicted on the religion became great, because with the introduction of cheap printing presses in Rangoon, their books and pamphlets were widely circulated. The distribution of wealth among the people in Lower Burma was beginning to lose its equilibrium, and the richer merchants and landlords showered the clergy with gifts of monasteries and goods, which were difficult to describe as "necessities" under the *Vinaya* rules. In some of the monasteries in Rangoon and Moulmein, brass bedsteads, mirrored wardrobes, polished dining tables and Western-styled cushioned chairs made their appearance, and some monks were even seen wearing yellow robes made of velvet. Indeed, more than in Upper Burma, the accusation of luxurious living leveled against the clergy was justified in British Burma.

NEW IDEAS AND NEW MANNERS. In Lower Burmese towns, by about the year 1870, a new generation of young men had grown up without having studied in a monastery. The initiation ceremony was still considered socially necessary for every young boy, but as the boys were now attending the government schools, they did not have the time and leisure to spend even one lent in a monastery as novices, and therefore it became the fashion for a young novice to don the yellow robe for only a week, during his terminal vacation from school. In the old days a boy took the initiation ceremony only at the age of fifteen or sixteen, because it marked the culmination of his elementary studies, but now that such studies were being pursued at the government school it was considered only logical that a boy should take his initiation any time between the ages of six and sixteen. Thus the initiation ceremony became purely a social event. As for the boy initiated, the occasion merely gave him the excuse to wear his hair in the new European style after it had started to grow again on his shaven head. In the short space of seven days he had learned nothing of monastic discipline.

In Rangoon, Moulmein, and Akyab, which were fast-growing ports, there were bright young men, some of whom had been educated in English schools in Calcutta, who were now serving as clerks in government offices or in the offices of European mercantile firms. They frequented horse races introduced by the European community, and at Rangoon especially it was considered fashionable for young people to go to the weekly meetings of the Rangoon Turf Club, to drink one or two pegs of whisky in the evening, and to denounce Buddhism as too old-fashioned, too pessimistic, and too illogical. Buddhist Sabbath days were no longer holidays. When all the offices closed at the end of each week on Sunday, being non-Christians they had no need to go to church, while, the day being of no importance in the Buddhist calendar, they had no desire to go to the monastery either. So Sunday was the day to go to the races and to eat and drink like Europeans. When the pendulum swung the other way as the result of the work of the great monks, the holding of the Fifth Great Synod and the re-crowning of the Shwedagon pagoda by King Mindon's embassy, there were new difficulties. Many of those bright young men, on returning to the fold, waxed puritanical and insisted that the monks should be more austere and that for the laity the Eight Precepts were not enough. To make up for their past neglect, some of the older clerks and civil servants took the lower ordination again but, as they were too old to begin studying the scriptures and too new to the monastic discipline, they flinched from taking the higher ordination. As old novices, their presence disturbed the even tenor of monastic life.

Conscious of the laity's demand for purity and austerity in the ranks of the clergy, some of the younger monks in the Lower Burmese towns formed themselves into a group of reformers, called the *Sulagandi* or the Junior Chapter. Their ideas were not new, as they borrowed freely from the new rules of conduct advocated by the Okpo Sayadaw. Their main aim was to belittle the authority of the ecclesiastical council over the monks of Lower Burma. The very name, the "Junior Chapter," was a challenge to the ecclesiastical council, because the sect suppressed by Bodawpaya's ecclesiastical council bore the same name. But that sect was known as *Sulagandi* because its members relied on the *Sulagandi*, a commentary on the *Vinaya* written in the twelfth century in Ceylon, to prove their case. However, the name "Junior Chapter" was now taken to mean that the younger monks were more pious than the older monks; if that contention was generally accepted, it could undermine the authority of the abbot and the senior monks in every monastery.

The revival of interest in the national religion also meant the revival of interest in national beliefs, customs and institutions. Among the newly rich families of the great ports, it became the fashion to imitate the dress and mannerisms of the royal palace at Mandalay, and to build monasteries and hold festivals on the grand scale of kings and queens. Native medicine and astrology also regained their popularity. Some of the more influential laymen started to use the title of "royal teacher" in addressing their favorite monks, although the latter had never even seen the king in person. All these developments corrupted many of the monks. Some monks felt pleased with the ostentation, the ceremonies, and the gifts; others tried to please their patrons by making astrological readings of horoscopes and prescribing mixtures and pills. Above all, many young monks left the order hoping to become rich overnight, and became traders, astrologers, and physicians.

THE THINGAZAR SAYADAW. One of the most famous among King Mindon's great monks was the Thingazar Sayadaw. He was born in May, 1815, at the village of Paukchaung near the small town of Paleik, some thirty miles from Amarapura, then the royal capital where King Bodawpaya's reign was drawing to a close. The boy was given by his parents the personal name of Maung Po or "Master More-than-Others," because of his unusual intelligence. He went to the village monastery at the age of six, but when his parents moved to Amarapura, some time later, he continued his studies at one of the great monasteries of that city. Proving to be a brilliant scholar, he was permitted to take the lower ordination at the age of thirteen, and was accepted as a pupil at one of the monastic colleges at Ava. On reaching the minimum age of twenty years in 1835, he took the higher ordination and became a wandering scholar, going from one monastery to another and studying at the feet of famous monks. He wrote a number of works on the scriptures, one of which was a commentary on the *Vinaya* rules. By 1850 he had become famous for his learning, and many monks came to study under him.

In the midst of his busy scholastic life he often retired to the forest sometimes spending a whole lent alone. His devoted followers among the laity built him monastery after monastery, but after residing in a monastery for two or three lents he would install the most senior among his pupils as abbot in his place, and would take to wandering again. King Mindon built for him a magnificent monastery at Mandalay and appointed him to the ecclesiastical council in 1860, but the great monk served for only a few years. Nonetheless, he remained very close to the king. An authority on the *Vinaya* rules, and ascetic far beyond the requirements of the monastic code, he was tolerant of human failings. He would not support the puritanic reforms proposed by the Ngettwin Sayadaw. A strict disciplinarian in his monasteries, he approved of King Mindon's efforts to purify the clergy, but at the same time he always was opposed to the excessive authority given to the ecclesiastical censor. Fearless and outspoken before the king, before the ecclesiastical council, and before congregations of monks or laymen, he had a sense of humor which, with his merry tales, drove his points home and won him deep affection and respect.

The Thingazar Sayadaw felt that the revived enthusiasm for the religion in Lower Burma should be guided and controlled in such a way that it would be able to withstand the shock of the final fall of the kingdom and survive under an alien government whose rule would extend all over the country. Accordingly he came down to Lower Burma in 1873 and visited the new religious centers of Rangoon, Prome, Henzada, Pegu, and Moulmein. He did not approve of the Okpo Sayadaw nor the Junior Chapter, but he advised and guided the abbots of the monasteries of Lower Burma to tighten the discipline of their monks. He won back many monks to his own Thudhamma sect. In his sermons to the laity he emphasized the importance of following the time-honored Buddhistic way of life, in spite of the changes in Burmese society resulting from political and economic causes. In 1882 he went on a pilgrimage to Buddhagaya and spent some time in Calcutta. Two years later he again went to India, with the purpose of going on to Ceylon, but the British authorities there denied him permission to proceed with the excuse that there was a famine on the island. He returned to Rangoon. While he was visiting Henzada, there was an attempt, which fortunately was not successful, on his life. Al- though the would-be assassin fired two bullets with a shotgun in full view of a congregation of some one thousand persons listening to the great monk giving his sermon, no arrest was made. It was generally presumed that some followers of the Okpo Sayadaw were behind the assassination plot. The Okpo Sayadaw himself denounced the action and came to worship the Thingazar Sayadaw in person. The Thingazar Sayadaw died in Moulmein in August, 1886, some nine months after the British annexation of the whole country.

THE MONK'S TALE. During Anawrahta's time the message of Buddhism reached the people through the *Jatakas* or "The Five Hundred and Fifty Stories" of the Buddha in his former existences, for Shin Arahan's monks used them in their sermons. The *Jatakas* constituted the layman's bible, for they were concerned not with the more advanced principles of Buddhism, "but with the general virtues, and inexorable law of *Karma*, according to which we reap as we sow, however many lives it may take for the reward or punishment to come to fruition." In the countless temples of Pagan, the *Jatakas* were also told to the people through paintings and sculptures, and in the intervening centuries these Birth Stories formed the subject of short stories, novels, poems, and plays performed both by living actors and by puppets. They were cited by the king's judges in support of their decisions. Many of the *Jatakas* were also transformed into folk tales. To cater to the Burmese love of fun and laughter and to keep the interest of the hearers who were already familiar with the actual story, the writer, the dramatist, or the lay preacher introduced comic characters and incidents into the original framework of a particular *Jataka* story which he was retelling. The monks, however, considered it improper to take such liberties with the text of the stories as given in the scriptures, and therefore they were at a disadvantage especially during King Mindon's time, when there was an influx of European fairy tales, short stories, and novels. In

Lower Burma, Burmese drama even abandoned its old tradition of using the *Jatakas* as the source of its plays.

The Thingazar Sayadaw invented a new literary form, the Monk's Tale. He still used the *Jatakas* in his formal sermons, but in short, informal addresses he usually narrated a short tale, which he made up on the spot. His model was the Burmese folk tale, and he reproduced in his own tales the gay and carefree atmosphere so characteristic of Burmese folk literature. However, as his tales dealt with the problems and difficulties that beset the clergy and laity of his day, the tales were satirical in aim and purpose. They were not fables in the strict sense of the term, for the moral lesson was not stated in so many words, but they drew the attention of his audiences to the religious controversies raging around them, and advised both the clergy and the laity to chart a careful course between the two extremes of laxity and puritanism in their religious practices. He was always careful that his satire and criticism of the follies and foibles of some of his contemporaries should be relieved by deft touches of humor, and he made his own noble order the butt of his jokes. Although Moulmein, Rangoon, and Mandalay at that time were inundated with pamphlets issued by the Christian missions attacking and ridiculing Buddhistic beliefs, the Thingazar Sayadaw never attacked or criticized other religions, for he was convinced that Buddhism in Burma could never be overwhelmed and destroyed by any attack from outside. His tales were so popular that some of the other great monks imitated him and told their own monk's tales. The second part of this collection includes some of the tales told by the imitators. The reader can see that delightful as they were, they could not equal the Thingazar Sayadaw's tales.

In telling his tales, the Thingazar Sayadaw had a subsidiary aim. Knowing full well that the end of the kingdom was swiftly approaching and realizing that Burmese society was being rapidly changed and altered, perhaps he wanted to preserve a picture of life in Burma as he knew it. To his listeners at Rangoon and Moulmein, many of whom had been seeing only the night before the latest Burmese play performed in a "permanent" theater, and some of whom were carrying pocket watches, the itinerant puppet show man and the spinster who waited for a young bachelor to call on her, described in the tales, were as quaint as the method of counting time by the crowing of the village cocks. Perhaps the very quaintness of the life depicted in the tales appealed to his listeners just as the long-drawn-out scene of a Burmese king in his audience chamber, which was a feature of the new Burmese drama, greatly attracted the Lower Burmese audiences. Thus, in addition to a full and faithful résumé and appraisal of the position of Burmese Buddhism on the eve of the British conquest, the tales contained vivid cameos of Burmese village life. By outsiders, Buddhism had often been criticized as a melancholy, gloomy, and pessimistic religion, but to neither the Burmese monk nor the Burmese layman had it ever been so. The very fact that these merry tales were told by one of the most pious of monks known to Burmese history, and were acclaimed by audiences of people whose devotion to their national religion had been freshly reawakened, illustrates this point. Whereas Burmese drama, under the shadow of impending doom for the nation, developed a new type of play and became saturated with sentimentality and pathos, the monk's tales never stooped to sentimentality, self-pity, or vain regrets. The predominant tone of the monk's tales was one of humor, good sense, and courage.

The monk's tales were always told by their author on the spur of the moment, and originally were not noted down by him or his listeners. By word of mouth they reached villages all over the country, and took their place alongside the *Jatakas*, the folk tales, and the law tales in the repertoire of the village storytellers. The first collection of the monk's tales was published in Burmese in 1911 by Saya Thein. His collection was very comprehensive and contained 161 tales by the Thingazar Sayadaw and 79 by the other great monks. However, many among them were not really tales but merely epigrams. Saya Thein, being a great Pāli scholar, retold the tales in too literary a tone and added to them his own learned quotations from the scriptures, so that in his collection they had a style quite different from the original used by the Thingazar Sayadaw. I first heard these tales from the lips of villagers when I was making my collection of Burmese folk tales and law tales, during the period 1926–29. The notes that I then took down were later submitted for comment and correction to my father who, as a boy at the government school at Rangoon, listened often to the Thingazar Sayadaw preaching. In the following pages I have endeavored to retell the monk's tales in their original style. Although I have rejected some of his tales and many of his prologues in favor of the relevant village versions, I have found Saya Thein's great collection to be of immense value. For the tales of other monks, I am entirely indebted to him, as they were not remembered elsewhere.

Tales by the
Thingazar Sayadaw

1. The Hungry Man from the Hills

Prologue: One of the most devoted patrons of the Thingazar Sayadaw was an extra assistant commissioner of Rangoon. He had been educated in an English school in Calcutta, and therefore he was not well versed in the scriptures as were his counterparts in Upper Burma. However, he was a devout Buddhist and built a monastery and invited the great monk to reside in it during the latter's many visits to Rangoon. Often he was exhorted by the venerable monk to give more attention to the actual practice of the religion, such as keeping the Sabbath on religious days. But the commissioner pleaded that under the British government those days were not holidays. The monk then suggested that he should treat Sundays as Buddhist Sabbath days, but then the official pleaded that because of his multifarious duties even Sundays were working days for him. Some years passed. The commissioner reached the age limit, and retired from the service of the British government on a pension. So, when the monk came again to Rangoon, he said, "Great layman, now you can keep the Sabbath regularly." "Alas, my lord," replied the layman, "I find that I cannot concentrate on religion, because my mind is never at rest, worrying about the welfare of my family." The learned monk smiled and remarked, "Great layman, you are like the Hungry Man from the Hills."

Once a Villager was making preparations to give a great feast and he invited, according to custom, all and sundry to take a share of his merit by helping in the building of a temporary hall of bamboo and thatch, in which alms would be offered to the monks. In response to the invitation, people from the neighboring villages came and took part, with skill and enthusiasm, in the building of the alms hall. Amidst the bustle and excitement, the Villager noticed a man from the hills who stood all alone watching the others doing the work, and with a sad expression on his face. So he went to him and asked kindly, "Man from the Hills, what ails you? Are you sick, are you ill?" "Sir," the Man replied sadly, "I want to work as the others are doing, I want to gain merit, and I want to join in the feast. But to my utter regret, I cannot do so. Who can work on an empty stomach?" On hearing this explanation, the Villager rushed into his kitchen, brought out a bowl of rice, a basin of vegetable soup, and a dish of fried chicken, and offered them to the Man from the Hills. Then he resumed his work together with the others. After a brief interval of time he looked towards the Man from the Hills, and he was surprised to see that the Man was again standing and watching the happy throng of workers with the same sad expression on his face. Greatly concerned, the Villager rushed to the Man and inquired what was the matter now. "Sir," the Man replied sadly, "I want to work as the others are doing, I want to gain merit, and I want to join in the feast. But to my utter regret, I cannot do so. Who can work on a full stomach?"

2. Gourd Is Forgotten and Gold Is Remembered

Prologue: On one of his many visits to Rangoon, the Thingazar Sayadaw was asked by a school principal whether it was really necessary to forsake the world and become a monk, or even to lead a life of austerity. "One needs to have only a clear conscience," the school principal argued, "and to remember religion at the moment of one's death." "That is very true," replied the Sayadaw. "However, unless a person actually practices his religion every day, his thoughts are likely to wander to mundane things at the moment of crisis, like Mr. Thin the Boatmaster."

In a village called "Above-the-Rocks," there lived a Boatmaster. He became very rich after many trading voyages down the river. But as he and his boat had to pass a stretch of rapids with protruding rocks, and as he did not know how to swim, instead of waxing fat with riches, he became pale and thin with anxiety. At last he conceived a brilliant plan. He bought a huge gourd and turned it into a bottle by emptying it of its contents. He kept this gourd bottle under his bed in the cabin of his boat. Now he felt safe and ceased to be in fear of drowning, for, should his boat ever capsize, he would float to safety clinging to this gourd.

Years passed, and the Boatmaster became fat although he continued to be known as Mr. Thin. But one day, as his boat was passing through the rapids after an unusually profitable voyage, it was caught in a storm and went out of control. But at that moment of crisis Boatmaster Thin did not remember the gourd but remembered instead the bag of gold lying in his cabin. "I will take my gold, my gold," he shouted to his boatmen. They thought he was talking about his gourd and, certain that he would float to safety on his gourd bottle, jumped into the river and swam ashore. But the poor Boatmaster remembered only to take the bag of gold, and, jumping into the water with it, he sank and was quickly drowned.

3. The Cucumber Alchemist

Prologue: Once, when the Thingazar Sayadaw was keeping lent at Myingyan, a town some fifty miles down the river from Mandalay, a harassed headman brought a quarreling couple before the great monk. "My lord," he explained, "this husband and that wife are quarreling and fighting every evening and the neighbors want me to arrest them for a breach of the peace. But I know their history and their circumstances, and so I have brought them to my lord for advice and counsel. The husband does no work at all, but the wife is a hawker of sweetmeats. He used to be a good farmer, until he became interested in alchemy, and now he spends all his time carrying out alchemic experiments. As chemicals are expensive, he has wasted all their savings, and now he squanders the daily earnings of his wife on this mad pursuit of the 'Philosopher's Stone.' I have tried to reason with him many times, but he insists that he will become a successful alchemist because an astrologer has so foretold." The Sayadaw smiled and narrated the following tale.

In a village, not many miles away from Mount Popa, the ancient home of magic and alchemy, there lived an Opium-Eater, who believed that one day he would receive the "Philosopher's Stone" as a gift from the guardian gods of the mountain. He boasted of this belief to his friends whenever they remonstrated with him on his opium habit, with the result that they decided to play a trick on him. So one afternoon, as he lay half asleep and half awake after a bout of opium eating, a friend walked stealthily and silently into his bedroom, and whispered fervently into his ear, "Keep your eyes shut and listen. I am a guardian god of Mount Popa, and I have come to tell you how to become a successful alchemist. You have heard of alchemists who experiment with mercury, alchemists who experiment with iron, and alchemists who experiment with runes, but you shall be the first Cucumber Alchemist. Take a bitter cucumber and grind it. Then mix it with a tical's weight of jaggery and a tical's weight of salt. Finally, swallow the mixture holding your breath, and you will find yourself a Cucumber Alchemist." When the effects of the opium were over, the Opium-Eater left the house swiftly, and, after buying the ingredients necessary for the wonderful mixture, and faithfully following the god's instructions, prepared and swallowed it. Then he decided that as he was now a successful alchemist he could no longer stay in the abode of human beings but must retire to the forest. Dressing himself in white as befitted one who had forsaken the world, he walked the few miles to the woodlands on the slopes of Mount Popa, reaching there at dawn.

In another village there was sorrow and misery. A young woman had married, against the wishes of her parents, a man who was a drunkard. The marriage proved to be a failure, and in shame and disappointment the young woman came alone to the woodlands and hanged herself from a tree just a few minutes before our Cucumber Alchemist arrived on the scene. "Indeed, I am an alchemist" exclaimed the Opium-Eater, "for here is a fruit-maiden, lovely and juicy. We alchemists cannot make love to human women, because they are meat-eaters and they stink, and so we make love to fruits having the shape of lovely maidens. It is fortunate for me that there are no other alchemists about to rob me of this lucky find." So, in great glee, he cut the rope and embraced the dead body. At this moment the young woman's father, uncle, and husband came running, searching for her. They saw the dead body in the arms of the Opium-Eater and snatched it away, at the same time beating and kicking him. "Brothers, brothers," protested the Opium-Eater, "you are alchemists of mercury, iron, and runes, whereas I am an alchemist of mere cucumber. I am no match for you, and so take her away, take her away."

4. A Cure for Asthma

Prologue: An old man came to attend a ceremony at the monastery where the Thingazar Sayadaw was staying. He met the Sayadaw and said, "My lord, I am never able to come and listen to your lordship's sermons, because I am so busy with my alchemic experiments. Unlike that of other alchemists, my aim is not to turn base metals into gold, but to discover the elixir of life which will keep me alive until the next Buddha appears. I shall then be able to worship him in person and listen to his preaching. My wife, of course, comes and listens to your lordship's sermons most eagerly, and I attend to my alchemy with similar avidity. Although our ways are different, our goal is the same, namely, Nirvana." The Sayadaw smiled and remarked, "Layman, if you do get to Nirvana as the result of your alchemy, you can say with the Village Physician, 'My medicine may be filthy, but it does cure my patients of their asthma.'

A Village Physician, poring over an old parchment book, found the following prescription: "Specific for asthma: one inch of elephant hide, boiled together with five ticals of garlic." He was impressed with the prescription and used it in the treatment of two or three asthma patients in his village. The patients recovered, and his fame spread to the neighboring villages. He was called to the bedside of asthma patients who lived many miles away. His fees were high but he was too mean to buy himself a bullock-cart. He was strong and wiry, but he was too nervous to ride on a horse. So he made his rounds every day on foot. This mode of traveling proved to have two distinct disadvantages for him. His expensive sandals made of cowhide became worn out in no time, and had to be replaced by others. His medicine bag, heavier than the bags of other physicians, because it had to contain a large piece of elephant hide, weighed him down and tired him. At last, he thought of a solution to his troubles. He bought a pair of sandals made of elephant hide, which lasted much longer than sandals made of cowhide. It was now no longer necessary for him to carry a large piece of elephant hide in his bag, because he could always cut off the needed inch of medicine from his sandals.

Some years passed, and there was not a single case of asthma which the Village Physician could not cure. Then, one day, in his own village, a fastidious old woman became stricken with asthma. The Physician was called in and he gave her his usual medicine for asthma, namely, an inch of elephant hide boiled with five ticals of garlic. The same evening, the Village Physician came to the bedside of his patient, fully expecting to find her cured. To his surprise and disappointment, he found the patient still struggling for breath. So he repeated the dose, but the patient showed no improvement. Thereupon, on the morning of the next day, he gave her a third dose of his medicine. He was very cross when he came in the evening and found the old woman still being racked with asthma. "You stubborn old woman," he scolded. "I have fed you with full three inches of elephant hide and still you have not recovered." Picking up one of his sandals, he angrily pointed out to her the place where the three inches had been cut off. "Take away your filthy sandal!" the old woman shouted. "It has trodden on dunghills and cesspools." "Do not be so fastidious," the Physician retorted. "The fact remains you have swallowed full three inches of the filthy sandal." The old woman was now seized with a nausea, on realizing that she had eaten a part of the dirty sandal, and soon she was vomiting freely. As a result of repeated vomiting, her lungs became clear and she was now fully cured.

The Village Physician later asked the old woman for his fee. "Your filthy medicine did not cure me at all," the old woman argued. "It was my vomiting that cured my asthma." "But you vomited because you loathed my medicine," the Physician insisted. "In any case, you are now cured of your asthma and I am entitled to my fee."

5. The Head-Clerk Who Could Not Wait for the Dawn

Prologue: It was a full-moon day, and the Thingazar Sayadaw gave the vows of the Eight Precepts to a huge congregation from the town of Moulmein. He noticed among the crowd a number of young clerks, who had obviously never received any monastic education. "Laymen," advised the Sayadaw, "ponder carefully on each of the Eight Precepts that you have just vowed to keep. In many ways you are like young herdsmen who have been put in charge of their fathers' cattle. As you know, there are three types of such herdsmen, namely, the careful, the careless, and the callous. The careful herdsman counts his cattle every hour so that he knows at once when any animal has strayed; the careless one never counts his cattle and therefore does not know whether any of his animals has strayed or not; and the callous herdsman actually lets the animals stray and will take a caning from his father, so that he will never be asked to herd cattle again. In the same way, some of you will keep the Sabbath zealously or conscientiously, while others will break their vows without realizing that they have done so. But I hope that there is no one among you who will break his vows deliberately as did the Head-Clerk who could not wait for the dawn."

The Head-Clerk of a district court in a Lower Burmese town was a hearty worker and also a hearty eater. His wife was very religious and fasted on every Sabbath day, but he himself was too busy with his work. There was a revival of interest in religion, and groups or associations were formed to sweep and wash the platforms of the pagodas in town, to hold religious discussions in the evenings, and to keep the Sabbath on full-moon days. The junior clerks were very enthusiastic, but could not prevail upon the Head-Clerk to join them in their religious activities. One full-moon day, however, the Head-Clerk found that he was the only person in the district office who was not going to the monastery to keep the Sabbath. A very junior clerk went to him and said, "Sir, you are our leader in our daily work, so why will you not be our leader in our religious work also?" Feeling embarrassed, he also went to the monastery, and together with his fellow clerks and his wife he took the vows of the Eight Precepts. The whole day the group remained in the monastery, telling the beads and reciting extracts from the scriptures. The Head-Clerk maintained a serious expression, but by the afternoon he felt the pangs of hunger.

At nightfall the Sabbath-keepers left the monastery for their respective homes, where they all continued their recitation of extracts from the scriptures before retiring. However, the Head-Clerk was interested only in his hunger, and the moment he and his wife reached home the following dialogue ensued:

HEAD-CLERK: Mistress of my household, please stop your recitation for a moment and please lay the table for my dinner.

WIFE: Master of the house, have you forgotten that both of us have been away at the monastery the whole day and therefore no dinner has been cooked?

HEAD-CLERK: But I shall soon die of hunger. Surely in the kitchen there is some food left over from this morning's breakfast?

WIFE: There is only some rice left, but why should you eat it now? You have kept the Sabbath the whole day and only the night remains. At dawn I shall get up and cook a wonderful meal for you to break your fast.

The Head-Clerk became silent and forced himself to fall asleep. But he woke up at midnight with a pain in his stomach and asked his wife to get up and cook his breakfast. The following dialogue resulted:

WIFE: It is some four hours to dawn and you should be man enough to be patient. Think of the merit that you will gain by keeping your vows, and think also of the grins and the jeers with which your clerks will greet you in the morning, when they come to know that you have failed to keep the Sabbath. You are not a child, you are a clerk in an important position, and in charge of the district court.

HEAD-CLERK: Why should the clerks know? Am I not master of my home? And what I do at home surely does not concern my fellow clerks at the court? I was a fool indeed to have permitted myself to be persuaded by those young fellows to keep the Sabbath.

WIFE: Husband, even as we talk, time is swiftly passing, and the golden dawn is on its way. This is the first time you have kept the Sabbath, and think of the merit and happiness you will gain in a few hours when you will have fulfilled your vows.

HEAD-CLERK: I do not desire any merit, and as to happiness, I was always happy until I took the vows to keep the Eight Precepts. So please stop your sermon and get up and cook my breakfast.

WIFE: Courage! The night cannot last forever.

The Head-Clerk remained silent, but after a few moments he jumped up and said, "I cannot wait any longer. This terrible night will surely last until the end of the universe." He then rushed headlong into the kitchen, put his hand into the rice-pot, and proceeded to eat the stale rice with relish and relief.

6. The Puppet Master Who Yawned Away the Night

Prologue: A group of young officials came to the monastery at Moulmein where the Thingazar Sayadaw was residing, and announced their intention of spending their vacation of seven days in fasting and meditation. The Sayadaw praised them for their piety and assigned them some rooms to live in. On the third or fourth day of their sojourn in the monastery the Sayadaw asked them, "Are you finding your stay here profitable? Would you have enjoyed your vacation better if you had stayed at home?" "We do find our stay here very profitable," replied the young officials, "but we miss our wives and children. To tell the truth, my lord, we find life here a little dull." The Sayadaw smiled and said, "You must be longing for the end of the vacation. You remind me of the Puppet Master Who Yawned Away the Night."

An Apprentice in a puppet show wanted to win fame and fortune as a Puppet Master and later even as a Puppet Showman. He had completed three long years of apprenticeship. As a junior apprentice he had spent two full years manipulating animal puppets. As a senior apprentice he had spent one full year manipulating the alchemist, the dragon, and the ogre puppets. He felt he was entitled to be given his mastership in puppetry and called upon to manipulate one of the puppets representing the main characters of a play. So he said to the Puppet Showman, "Master Showman, I have spent full three years under you as an apprentice, manipulating the subsidiary puppets. I venture to think that I have fully mastered the art of puppetry." To his disappointment the Master Showman replied, "My boy, be patient. Spend another year as an apprentice."

Another year passed and again the Apprentice went before the Showman, and asked to be given his mastership. The Showman did not think that the Apprentice was ready for promotion. But, on the other hand, he did not want to disappoint him again. After due consideration he hit upon a compromise. So he said, "All right, my boy, you have won your mastership. Tonight I will assign you a puppet important to the play." The newly made Puppet Master spent the whole day in a state of great excitement, trying to guess what particular puppet he would be asked to manipulate. Evening came, the orchestra played, and the animal puppets appeared and gave their dances. Then the alchemist, dragon, and ogre puppets appeared, and gave their dances. Finally, the play of the evening began. The new Puppet Master, on being assigned a puppet representing the King of the Gods, dreamed of making his mark that very night. However, as he listened to the synopsis of the play, he learned that throughout the play the King of the Gods merely sat and watched the other characters. So throughout the night the poor Puppet Master merely held the puppet upright, and, repeatedly yawning, he awaited eagerly the coming of the dawn and the end of the performance.

7. The Novice Who Jeered at the Sabbath-Keepers

Prologue: When the Thingazar Sayadaw was on a visit to Pyinmana, a town in Middle Burma, hundreds of people came to him, and, as it was a Sabbath day, they took the formula of the Eight Precepts from him. Although they were enthusiastic and devout, they were obviously in a holiday mood, and the Sayadaw exhorted them to behave with the dignity and decorum befitting keepers of the Sabbath, and to spend the afternoon in silence, in meditation, and in prayer. To illustrate his point, he told the tale of the Novice who jeered at the Sabbath-Keepers.

It was a full-moon day, and the good ladies of the village had come to the monastery, bringing alms food. They ceremoniously offered the alms food to the Abbot, took from him the formula of the Eight Precepts, and then retired to sit in the shade of the mango and tamarind trees in the courtyard of the monastery. Inside the monastery the Abbot and the monks recited the scriptures. But the little Novice had nothing to do. Because it was a Sabbath day, there were no lessons for him. So he strolled about the courtyard.

Casually, the Novice gave a glance at the good ladies resting under the trees, and he was surprised to see that instead of sitting and meditating or saying their prayers or telling their beads, they were talking to each other. Thinking that they were discussing some religious or moral subject, he went near them and listened carefully, and he heard the following conversation:

FIRST LADY: Do you think that the price of oil will go up next month?

SECOND LADY: Of course it will, and my husband is so sure of making a huge profit on the sale of his stock of oil that he has promised to buy me another pair of gold bangles.

THIRD LADY: Tell your husband not to be cheated by the goldsmith. Last month I bought a pair of gold bangles from him, and I am sure the gold was not up to standard.

FOURTH LADY: I do not think that the poor fellow is really dishonest. His heart has not been in his work since his second daughter eloped with an apprentice.

The little Novice went on listening, and the topic of conversation changed from elopements to marriages, then to sons-in-law, then to family quarrels, then to lawsuits, then to partitions of family estates, then to the price of land, then to the price of gold, and then back again to the price of oil. By that time the sun had set, and as the good ladies prepared to leave the monastery and go home, the little Novice went to the gate and sat on the gatepost.

The good ladies, as they passed through the gate, said to the little Novice "We have spent a good day, for we have kept the Sabbath. So little Novice, accept a share of our merit." To their surprise, the little Novice did not give the usual reply of "Good, good, I accept a share of your merit"; instead he shouted, "Boo, boo, woo, woo!" The good ladies felt insulted, and, rushing back to the Abbot, they asked that the Novice be punished for his rude behavior.

The Abbot felt very angry, and, seizing a cane in his hand, he called to the Novice to come and receive his punishment. "But, my lord," pleaded the little Novice. "They were not really keeping the Sabbath, but were discussing various matters." Then he proceeded to repeat the entire conversation between the good ladies which he overheard during the afternoon. The Abbot listened with open mouth. When the Novice finished speaking, the Abbot gave a great sigh, threw away his cane, and, turning to the good ladies, he also shouted, "Boo, boo, woo, woo!"

8. Mistress Cold Who Sold Pickled Fish

Prologue: When the Thingazar Sayadaw arrived at a town in Lower Burma for a short stay, he was received by some five hundred devotees. After he had been taken to a monastery, he was asked to give a sermon. "It is not a Sabbath day," replied the Sayadaw, "and many of the laymen and laywomen present must have come merely to greet me, and are now anxious to go back to their work. I shall be here for some days and you will have many opportunities to listen to my preaching. If I should give a sermon now, many of you would find yourselves behaving as Mistress Cold, the Pickled Fish Seller did, while listening to a long sermon."

Mistress Cold earned her living by hawking pickled fish round the village. One afternoon, while beginning her usual round, she passed by a house where an initiation ceremony was being held. As she watched, the Abbot presiding over the ceremony started to give his sermon. Mistress Cold thought to herself, "Engrossed in my business of selling pickled fish, I have been neglecting my religion. The sun is still high, and surely there is time for me to listen to the words of wisdom of the venerable Abbot."

At first Mistress Cold found the sermon interesting and instructive, but, as the Abbot continued to drone out his sermon, she became restless, for the sun was rapidly going down. She kept glancing at the Abbot, at the sun, and at her tray of pickled fish, covered up and hidden by her shawl. "I have not sold even a viss," she said to herself with great anxiety, "and should the sermon continue, it will be too dark for me to go round the village." Moments passed and still the Abbot went on preaching. She looked around, hoping to see some of the guests slipping out of the hall, so that she could follow them. But all seemed to be engrossed in the sermon. She became feverish with anxiety.

At long last, the sermon was finished. The Host stood up, and, beating a gong, shouted out, "In this our deed of merit may all beings take a share!" Poor Mistress Cold, in her anxiety and excitement, forgot where she was and, standing up, she also shouted, "Pickled fish! Pickled fish! Only a quarter piece for a viss! Who will buy my pickled fish?"

9. The Mother Who Wept with Her Son-in-Law

Prologue: While the Thingazar Sayadaw was residing at Moulmein, a group of elders from a remote village up the Salween river came and said, "My lord, after hearing your lordship's sermons we decided to revive the religion in our village. So we built a monastery, and we invited some monks to reside there, but one by one they went away leaving the monastery empty." So the Sayadaw deputed one monk from among his retinue to become the residing monk of that village. Some months later the Sayadaw visited Moulmein again and the same elders again came and pleaded that the Sayadaw should depute another monk, because the previous monk had left the monastery suddenly and without explanation. Again, the Sayadaw deputed one of his retinue to go along with the elders. Some months passed, the Sayadaw was again in Moulmein, and the elders from the remote village, reporting that the second monk after a few weeks had left their monastery suddenly and without explanation, begged for yet another monk. Accordingly, the Sayadaw deputed another from among his retinue. On the Sayadaw's next visit to Moulmein, the elders came again and pleaded, "My lord, we are indeed very sorry to inform your lordship that our monastery has become empty again, as your third pupil also left our village suddenly and without giving his reasons." "Esteemed laymen," replied the Sayadaw, "I can only weep like the Mother who wept together with her Son-in-Law."

In a village there once lived a Farmer and his Wife who had three beautiful daughters. One day a very handsome young man by the name of Easy-Life came and offered to serve as an apprentice on the farm for three years. The Father found him industrious and skillful, and the Mother found him obedient and considerate. Therefore, at the end of the three years' period of apprenticeship, they were very reluctant to let him go. Then the Mother had a brilliant idea and married the eldest daughter to Easy-Life. Unfortunately, the daughter died soon afterwards. At the funeral Master Easy-Life lamented:

"How can I live without you?
All is woe! All is woe!
And now where shall I go?"

The Mother, hearing him crying thus, joined him in his lamentation and wept aloud:

"All is woe! All is woe!
  But please do not go,
  For there is the second one."

So Master Easy-Life continued working on the farm, and after a decent interval the Mother married him to the second daughter. But misfortune again befell the family and the second daughter also died. At the funeral, Master Easy-Life lamented as before:

"How can I live without you?
  All is woe! All is woe!
  And now where shall I go?"

The Mother, as before, wept with him and cried loudly:

"All is woe! All is woe!
  But please do not go,
  For there's the third one."

So Master Easy-Life continued working on the farm, and after a decent interval the mother married him to the third daughter. But alas, she also died soon afterwards. At the funeral Master Easy-Life wailed as before:

"How can I live without you?
  All is woe! All is woe!
  And now where shall I go?"

The Mother, as on the previous occasions, joined in. But she now cried loudly:

"Are you a tiger that has devoured my daughters?
  Are you a snake that has swallowed them all?
  All is woe! All is woe!
  But this time, out you go."

10. The Monastery-Donor
Who Had His Eyes Washed

Prologue: During one of his tours of Lower Burma, the Thingazar Sayadaw was approached by a layman for his intervention in the matter of a wayward monk. "My lord," explained the layman, "in the monastery of my village there resides a bogus monk. All the villagers respect him, for he seems so pious and venerable. But a fortnight ago I caught him holding the hand of a servant maid who had brought him some alms food from her mistress." "Layman," asked the Thingazar Sayadaw, "were there witnesses?" "No, my lord," replied the layman. "It was not a Sabbath day, and it was nearly noon, so the monastery was deserted." "Layman," advised the Sayadaw with a smile, "without adequate evidence never make an accusation against a monk, for, if you do, your eyes will be washed with the juice of the tobacco leaf mixed with salt."

Merchant and his Wife had saved much money and, as they had no children, they decided to retire from business and devote their time to religion. They built a fine monastery and installed a learned and venerable monk as the Abbot. They also invited many young monks to come and reside in the monastery. This deed of merit received the acclaim of their fellow villagers, who conferred upon them the customary title of "Donors of a Monastery."

The Merchant now known as "Monastery-Donor," became a vegetarian and started to lead a life of strict austerity. On every religious day he invited the Abbot, the other monks, the novices, the lay brothers, and all the young boys residing in the monastery to his house and offered them breakfast. However, as he himself was a vegetarian he served only vegetable dishes. The Abbot, although old in learning and also in years, was still stout and strong and the others were young; it was therefore only natural that they should, after a time, find the food dull and monotonous. One religious day the Monastery-Donor saw to his consternation that the Abbot was absent from the usual breakfast. He anxiously inquired why the Abbot was absent, but the monks, the novices, the lay brothers, and the boys remained silent. As the Monastery-Donor repeated his question, one lay brother replied gruffly that the Abbot was slightly indisposed. The Monastery-Donor, upbraiding the lay brother for leaving the Abbot ill and infirm, ran headlong to the monastery. But as he reached the gates he composed himself and walked softly towards the Abbot's chamber, for, he thought to himself, the venerable monk might have fallen asleep after a restless night and so should not be disturbed. Reaching the Abbot's chamber, he stealthily pushed open the door, but there was no sign of the old monk. Sick with anxiety, he went from room to room until he finally entered the kitchen. There he saw a shocking sight. The Abbot was sitting bolt upright in front of the oven, eating with relish some fried eggs from a steaming frying pan.

Disappointed and dismayed, the Monastery-Donor rushed back to his house and collapsed at the feet of his Wife shouting, "The Abbot is frying eggs, the Abbot is frying eggs! I saw with my own eyes, the Abbot is frying eggs!" "That is ridiculous," argued the Wife. "How can you accuse our venerable teacher of breaking the precept against the taking of life?" "All the same, he was frying eggs," insisted the Monastery-Donor. "I saw with my own eyes, he was frying eggs." The Wife called out to the neighbors for help, explaining that some evil spirit or witch, out of jealousy for his deeds of merit, had cast a spell on the Monastery-Donor, causing him to become delirious. The neighbors came running in, and, as the Monastery-Donor still kept on shouting, "I saw with my own eyes, he was frying eggs," they became certain that he was under a spell. So they seized hold of him, and resorted to the usual cure for delirious and bewitched persons; they put into his eyes the juice of the tobacco leaf mixed with salt, until he stopped shouting. Although the Monastery-Donor had to become silent because his eyes were smarting, he was by no means appeased. He waited patiently until nightfall, and then in the privacy of their bedchamber he said to his Wife, "Foolish woman, I saw with my own eyes, he was frying eggs." His Wife looked at him in alarm and anxiety and sighed, "Alas, the attack has come back again, and I must call in the neighbors." The Monastery-Donor heard her words and, fearing another eyewash, he whispered meekly, "All right, all right, he was not frying eggs."

11. The Shaven-Head
Who Preferred Pork to Cabbage

Prologue: While the Sayadaw was on a visit to Moulmein, a poorly dressed person came and invited the great monk to come to his humble cottage for alms food the following morning. He explained that he was a laborer in the nearby sawmill. At that moment, an opulent-looking personage arrived, attended by two or three servants. Introducing himself as a timber merchant, he also invited the great monk to come to his newly built brick house for alms food the following day. "But I have just invited our teacher for the same morning," protested the laborer. The merchant glared at him and said airily. "The Teacher will have better food at my house." The Sayadaw intervened before the argument could develop into an open quarrel. "Great Layman," he said to the merchant, "the rules of our order require that I accept the first invitation and, moreover, should I break the rule, I shall be called the Shaven-Head who preferred Pork to Cabbage."

I t was the morning of a religious day, but, as the Monk sat and waited, no one came bringing alms food. He had not gone on his daily begging round in the village because, as it was a religious day, he fully expected that some villager would come to keep the Sabbath in the monastery, bringing some alms food. The lay brother was sick and could not cook. To make matters worse, the Monk was unduly hungry that particular morning.

He heard some footsteps and looked eagerly towards the doorway. A man from the western quarter of the village entered, and, after kneeling down and worshiping the monk, said, "Lord, please honor us by coming to our humble house and accepting some alms food." The monk, however, was not too overjoyed because he knew that as the layman before him was only a poor farmer; his alms food would consist only of rice and boiled cabbage. "Still, nice and cabbage is better than nothing," he consoled himself. However, just as the Monk was adjusting his robes to go forth, another man, this time from the eastern quarter of the village, entered, and, after kneeling down and worshiping, said, "Lord, please honor us by coming to our humble house and accepting some alms food." The Monk was in a quandary, for he knew the newcomer to be a rich Merchant, who always offered rice and curried pork as alms food. His mouth watered at the remembrance of the dishes of curried pork which he had tasted on previous occasions at the Merchant's house, and he said to himself bitterly, "Alas, too late by moments only."

Then the Monk suddenly thought of a way by which he could accept the Merchant's invitation. Turning round to the two villagers, he said, "As both of you have invited me to breakfast and as I can go to one house only, I must ask you, Merchant, to take hold of my right hand, and I must ask you, Farmer, to catch hold of my left hand. Then you must pull me from opposite directions, and the one who can pull me to his side will get me for breakfast." He suggested this tug of war because he thought that the Merchant was certain to win as he was the stouter of the two. The two laymen soon started the tug of war, but, to the alarm of the Monk, the Merchant, living an easy life, was out of condition and it became obvious that the wiry Farmer would soon emerge the winner. In desperation, the Monk gave a kick to the shin of the Farmer. The Farmer, in great pain and anger, let go of the Monk's left hand, with the result that Monk and Merchant fell on the floor on top of one another and with a loud bump. The Farmer, standing on one leg, gave vent to his feelings by singing the following ditty:

"Rebel against Cabbage,
    Struggling to join Pork,
    Go your way, Shaven-Head."

12. Lucky and Unlucky Days

Prologue: After the Thingazar Sayadaw had fixed the date of his departure from Mandalay for Moulmein, some of his followers pointed out that the proposed date, according to Burmese astrology, was an unlucky day. "A monk," replied the Sayadaw, "has no lucky or unlucky days. Those of you who do not agree with me should remember the case of the Southern and the Northern Abbots."

A village on the upper reaches of the river Irrawaddy had two monasteries, one at the southern end of the village, and the other at the northern end. Both were big monasteries with many monks, and there existed a feeling of rivalry between the two institutions. Both the Abbots were learned and pious, but the Abbot of the Southern Monastery was a great believer in astrology, whereas the Abbot of the Northern Monastery did not believe in astrology at all.

One day both the Abbots received invitations from the King at Ava to take part in a religious ceremony there. The Southern Abbot decided to leave for Ava the following day, because it was a lucky day. The Northern Abbot, on learning that his rival had chosen the following day as the date of his departure because it was a lucky day, announced that he would leave the village for Ava one day later as it was an unlucky day.

The following day the Southern Abbot and his followers left the village in a boat painted white, which was considered a lucky color. After the day's journey they stopped for the night at a village. The Headman of the village came down to the boat and said to the Abbot, "My lord, tomorrow I am holding an initiation ceremony for my little son, but unfortunately the Abbot of our village monastery was suddenly taken ill this afternoon and will not be able to attend the ceremony. As the golden city of Ava is only about three hours' journey from here, I beg your lordship to attend the ceremony and leave our village only at noon." The Southern Abbot accepted this invitation. Accordingly, when dawn came the Southern Abbot and his followers left their boat for the initiation ceremony at the Headman's house.

At that very moment, up the river the Northern Abbot and his followers started out on their journey to Ava, in a boat painted black, which was considered to be an unlucky color. A high wind suddenly blew and the boat traveled very swiftly, with the result that by noon it reached the village where the initiation ceremony was being held. The boat sailed past, but after an hour's journey, because of its great speed, it hit a rock and was wrecked. The Northern Abbot and his followers swam to safety, and, as they rested on the riverbank, his followers chided the Abbot thus: "My lord tempted the stars; my lord treated astrology with contempt; hence all this trouble." The Northern Abbot did not reply but gazed up the river with a remorseful look.

As the Northern Abbot stood gazing, he saw the white boat of the Southern Abbot approaching. It was going at a great speed and very soon it hit a rock and capsized. As the Southern Abbot and his followers swam to safety, the Northern Abbot turned to his followers and said, "Your grandfather yonder, in spite of his astrology, has done no better than I. The two of us will enter the King's audience chamber together looking like drowned rats."

13. Saturday-Borns

Prologue: When the Thingazar Sayadaw was visiting Henzada, an elderly man, who was an ardent admirer of the Okpo Sayadaw, said, "I listened to my lord's sermon the other night, and to my surprise, I found it to be of the same excellent standard as the sermons of the Okpo Sayadaw. Only this morning I found out that both my lord and the Okpo Sayadaw are Sunday-borns. Obviously, Sunday-borns are great teachers." The Sayadaw, displeased with the flattery, smiled and said "Layman, I will tell you about a great Abbot who was born not on a Sunday but on a Saturday."

In the golden city of Ava there once lived a famous Abbot. He was not only a great preacher but also a great teacher. The highest officials of the land, including the King himself, flocked to hear his sermons, and most of the other abbots in the great city had been his pupils at one time or another. Although learned and pious, he had two faults. First he was very short-tempered, and, second, he took pride in the fact that he was born on a Saturday.

One day the Queen held a great alms-giving ceremony, to which the Abbot was specially invited. After the monks had finished their meal, and the Abbot had given his sermon, the King, the Queen, the Ministers of State, and the Judges of the Supreme Court remained sitting while the palanquins were being called to take the monks back to their monasteries. The great Abbot said to the Queen, "Your Majesty can hold this great ceremony because you are a great Queen, and Your Majesty is a great Queen because you were born on a Saturday. Your Majesty's Consort, the great King himself, was born on a Saturday." Some of the Ministers joined in the conversation and said that they were Saturday-borns too. Many of the Judges were also found to be Saturday-borns. The Abbot feeling very pleased, commented, "We Saturday-borns always achieve greatness in various fields of life. You have become King and Queen, Ministers and Judges, and I have become a great Abbot."

Among the group of beggars waiting in the courtyard to receive the alms food left over by the monks was a Saturday-born, and he listened with interest to the Abbot's words. When the palanquins had arrived at the door, and the Abbot was getting into one of them, the Saturday-born Beggar came forward and said, "My lord, I am also a Saturday-born." The Abbot gave him an angry look and explained, "We were born on royal Saturdays, golden Saturdays, glorious Saturdays, whereas you were born on a begging Saturday, a tramping Saturday, a good-for-nothing Saturday."

14. Aloft the Plum Tree

Prologue: One morning, after the learned monks had eaten the alms food offered by him, King Mindon bewailed the fact that not one among his teachers had become an arahat. "My lords," said the king, "I build you fine monasteries and I offer you alms food regularly. In return, you do show me the way to piety, but I feel poorly recompensed, for no one among my lords has striven enough to reach the state of arahatship" All the other monks remained silent, but the Thingazar Sayadaw could not let the king's criticism pass unchallenged. "Your Majesty," he replied, "we are aloft the plum tree and you are criticizing us from the ground."

Two travelers were making a perilous journey. One was tall and strong, whereas the other was small and weak. They had to pass through, first, a forest full of thieves and robbers and, second, another forest full of tigers and leopards. Singlehanded, the Tall Man fought the violent robbers and the ferocious animals while the Small Man merely looked on. Then the two companions had to pass through a long stretch of waterless desert, and, when halfway across it, the Small Man lay down on the sand and moaned, "Brother, I can go no farther. So leave me here to die." But the Tall Man pointed towards a clump of trees in the distance and said, "Brother, we must be nearly through the desert, because yonder are some trees. Perhaps they are plum trees, in which case we can quench our thirst by sucking the juice of their plums." Encouraged by these words, the Small Man continued the journey, only to fall down again later, overcome by the heat and thirst.

The Tall Man picked up his exhausted companion and carried him in his arms until they reached the fringe of the desert and came to the trees. As the Tall Man had expected, they were plum frees. The Tall Man swiftly climbed one of the trees, but he found it difficult to pick the plums, as the branches were too thorny and brittle. As he paused aloft the plum tree, the Small Man shouted from below, "You lazy fellow, you cowardly fellow! You call yourself a man, yet you cannot even get a few plums!"

15. The Father and His Absent Sons

Prologue: In his golden palace King Mindon spent a restless night. A conscientious and humane king, he worried over his subjects who had migrated from the Mandalay region. When morning dawned he sent an invitation to the great monks, his royal teachers, to come to his palace and accept alms food. When the monks had come and eaten their breakfast, the king told them of his sleepless night. "My lords," he said, "those who went to other Burmese towns are still in my territory, and I worry for them. Those who went to the British territory are also my responsibility, because they are still Burmese by birth. I am now old and frail and soon I shall die. But I shall go to my death carrying upon my conscience the burden of failure and frustration, because I have done nothing for their welfare." The Thingazar Sayadaw, who was among the royal monks present, replied, "Great King, a man can but do his best and no more, and, besides you, every one of your subjects has a protector, namely, the Karma of his good deeds. Therefore, Your Majesty is worrying for nothing, as the Old Father worried over his two Absent Sons."

In a remote village at the foot of the Chin Hills, there once lived an Old Farmer with his two Sons. The three worked hard, but the soil was unfertile and water was scarce. They could produce only maize and a rice of very poor quality. At last the two Sons, after obtaining permission from the Father, left the village in search of wealth and comfort in more prosperous regions, The Elder Son went north to Bhamo near the Chinese frontier, while the Younger Son went south to Rangoon. After some years of endeavor, the Elder Son became a petty trader and he waxed fat, living on bacon and sausages brought in by the Chinese caravans. The Younger Son became a prosperous farmer and he also waxed fat, living on juicy and nutritious Lower Burmese rice. They forgot their Father in the old village, who, however, always remembered them with longing.

One day a party of adventurous pilgrims arrived to worship at an ancient pagoda in the old village, and, as they were rich merchants, they brought with them a large supply of bacon and sausages from Bhamo and nutritious Lower Burmese rice. The Old Farmer came to the pagoda in the evening as was his custom, and the pilgrims who were eating their dinner invited him to join them. After a few mouthfuls, he started to shed tears, and, on being asked by the anxious pilgrims to explain why he was crying, he replied, "Friends, I have never tasted such delicious food before and I wish that my two Sons were also here tonight to share in my good fortune. One is now in Bhamo and the other in Rangoon and I am sure they have never eaten such a good meal as this in their lives."

16. The Dead Monk without a Funeral Pyre

Prologue: After an offering of sumptuous food, King Mindon said to his royal monks, "My lords, I have donated for your use pleasant gardens and fine monasteries, and I have offered from time to time nourishing food, medicine, and robes. But, before I make further offerings, I may demand to know what meditative exercises you perform, so that I can be satisfied that my lords are on their speedy way to Arahatship." "Great King," replied the Thingazar Sayadaw, "we are obliged to Your Majesty for generous donations and offerings, but it would not be proper for us to bargain that we shall strive to become Arahats in exchange for Your Majesty's continued patronage. Your Majesty may discontinue making offerings to us, but we cannot report to Your Majesty our daily doings, for we are not dead monks without funeral pyres."

The old Abbot of a village monastery had died, and his successor wanted to honor him by giving him a great funeral. The villagers came forward with offers to contribute to the cost of various items of the funeral, for example, the gilded coffin, the alms food not only for monks but for all comers to the funeral, the theatrical shows, but no one came forward with an offer to contribute to the cost of the most expensive item, namely, the magnificent funeral pyre. The new Abbot kept the dead body lying in state for several weeks, but still no donor of the funeral pyre appeared. Although the dead body was carefully embalmed, the villagers began to comment adversely on the long period of time during which it was being exposed to the public gaze. The new Abbot reluctantly closed the coffin, but he did not lose hope.

Time passed, and preparations for the funeral were nearly completed, but still no donor of the funeral pyre had come forward. In desperation, the new Abbot approached some of the more wealthy villagers, but they regretted that they had not enough money to build the funeral pyre. Then one day a Merchant from a nearby town came to the monastery and said, "My lord Abbot, I understand that you are still waiting for someone to build the funeral pyre. I have made a huge profit on my last business venture and I want to spend it on some charity." "It will indeed bring much merit to you, Layman," replied the Abbot with great enthusiasm. "But before I make the donation," the Merchant continued, "I must know the age of the dead Abbot, the names of his parents, the color of his complexion, his exact height, and the exact time of his death." "Layman," the Abbot cried out in anger, "either you build the funeral pyre or leave the monastery before I drive you out! The dead monk can remain without a funeral pyre, and I will not answer your stupid questions."

17. To Each His Own Foot

Prologue: King Mindon said to the Thingazar Sayadaw: "My lord, at the full-moon feast of Tazaungmon, special offerings of alms food are made to the pagodas by the people. Some make the offerings at dawn on the full-moon day itself, while others make the offerings before midnight the previous evening. I consider that the second practice is wrong, because alms food is offered to monks only in the morning. Therefore, I intend to issue a proclamation, prohibiting the offering of alms food to the pagodas before dawn." "Your Majesty," the Sayadaw replied, "when one offers alms food to a monk, it is meant to be eaten, and as a monk eats only in the morning, one makes the offering before noon. In contrast, when one makes an offering of alms food to a pagoda or an image of the Buddha, it is meant merely as a token of worship. Your Majesty must realize that people have their own reasons and own difficulties, which outsiders may not know. Thus, a person who makes his offering of alms food to a pagoda before dawn perhaps does so because he has some work to perform in the morning, even though it is a full-moon day, and will not be able to come to the pagoda then. As long as he makes the offering with real devotion, it does not matter whether it is done at dawn or the previous midnight. As the Mouse said to the Elephant, "To each his own foot."

An Elephant and a Mouse met in the forest one afternoon and narrated to each other their adventures. The Elephant said, "I am the king of the forest, and ordinarily I never run away from the enemy. But today I met a rogue elephant, and, wanting to avoid battle with him, I turned round and ran under some trees. The trees were not high enough, and a branch made a deep gash on my back. If you will look, you will see that it is fully two feet long."

"Doubtless it is a painful wound," said the Mouse. "But, my friend, you were never in danger of your life because, first, the rogue elephant could not have killed you and, second, the tree branch could never have reached your heart. With me, it was different. Only an hour ago I was chased by a wild cat, and was nearly caught. He gave a jab with his claws, and nearly ripped open my side. If you will look, you will see a gash at least two feet long."

The Elephant looked at the Mouse, and smiled. "My friend," he said, "I am not saying that you are a liar, but I may point out that your whole body from tip to tail is not even one foot in length. Then how can you say that your wound is two feet long?"

"Great animal," the Mouse replied, "to each his own foot. You measure the length of your gash by your big foot and I measure mine by my own small foot."

18. The Hillman's Revenge

Prologue: After the Thingazar Sayadaw had finished his meal of alms food at the palace of the Crown Prince, the Crown Princess, who was also a very famous poetess, said bitterly, "My lord will notice that my husband is not present today. In fact, he has not come home for the last three or four nights. All day he is absorbed in his work at the Supreme Court, and at night he is busy with his many mistresses. He is a great judge, but he is most unjust to me. He is a king's son, but I am also a king's daughter; he is the lord of Kanaung Town, but I am also the lady of Hlaing Town; he is a great soldier, but I am also a great musician; he is a great scholar, but I am also a great poetess. So, my lord, I should be free from all blame and criticism if I decide to neglect him and even become unfaithful to him in revenge." The Sayadaw smiled and replied, "I will give a good scolding to the Crown Prince this very afternoon, but Princess, remember the Hillman and his Revenge."

A Burmese Merchant was in the habit of visiting various market towns in the hill regions on business, and during one such trip he was stricken with malaria. For days he lay unconscious or delirious, and he was patiently nursed by a Hillman and his family. At last he recovered, and, when he was strong enough to travel again, he said, "My friend Hillman, you and your family have saved my life; I will now go back to my village on the Irrawaddy river. You must come and visit me and stay at my house as my honored guest for several days."

The following summer the Hillman decided to take a vacation from his work and go and visit his friend in the plains. So, riding his favorite horse, he journeyed down the passes to his friend's village. He was received with great pleasure by the Merchant, who greeted him with these words: "My benefactor, my friend, my brother, all I have is yours, and so stay here with me forever." The Hillman was also introduced to the neighbors, and after a few days he became so popular that he had to spend most of his time visiting them by turns.

After some days the Merchant said to the Hillman, "You spend your time visiting the neighbors, and I feel so lonely without you. May I borrow your horse so that I can visit my relations in the nearby villages?" The Hillman willingly lent the horse. The Merchant was an inconsiderate fellow, and so he rode the horse from sunrise to sunset for three days in succession, with the result that the poor animal became quite lame.

The Hillman was greatly angered by the unkind treatment meted out to his beloved horse and swore to himself that he would have his revenge. "If he ill-treats my horse, I will ill-treat his boat," he murmured to himself. So, hiding his anger, he spoke sweetly to the Merchant and borrowed the latter's boat. From sunrise to sunset, for three days in succession, the Hillman rowed the boat up and down the river, with the result that his hands became swollen with plying the oars. Finding that revenge after all was not sweet, he bade a hasty farewell to the Merchant and left for the hills leading his lame horse.

19. The Monk and the Dwindling Tiger

Prologue: After offering some alms food to the Thingazar Sayadaw, a group of laymen said, "My lord, we beg you to give us a 'fan-down' sermon." "Good Laymen," replied the Sayadaw, "I will give you a sermon, but it is neither formal nor informal, neither 'fan-up' nor 'fan- down.' A sermon is a sermon, no more, no less. It is the lay people of Lower Burma who invented these new terms, 'fan-up' or 'formal' sermon and 'fan-down' or 'informal' sermon. But we monks are also to be blamed, because we usually dance to the tune called by the laymen. As a result, we often appear very foolish, as in the case of the Monk and his Dwindling Tiger."

Once there lived a Monk who was not too learned. His sermons were very boring to listen to, and there came a time when no one offered him alms food. So he migrated to another village, but, benefiting from his previous experience, he did not go to the village monastery but resided in a makeshift monastery of bamboo and thatch on the edge of a small forest. As forest-dwelling monks were believed to be taking advanced meditative exercises, they were never expected to give any sermon, and the villagers flocked to the forest monastery, bring offerings of alms food and robes.

After some weeks, some of the villagers begged the Monk not to expose himself any further to the ferocious animals of the forest, but to come and dwell in the village monastery. But the Monk prudently remained in the forest. The fame of the forest-dwelling monk spread to the neighboring villages, and more and more people visited him and begged of him to come and dwell in their village monasteries. Then the Monk thought to himself, "I must please my followers in some way or other. I must either go and reside in their monastery, or agree with them that there are wild animals in the forest, although I have come across none." So when some villagers again came and insisted that he should no longer expose himself to the ferocious animals of the jungle, he replied, "Yes, yes, Laymen, only last night I saw a tiger under yonder tree, but I will risk my life to complete my meditative exercises." This remark made the Monk even more popular and he received more and more alms food and robes.

There was a mischievous fellow among the villagers and he, after a time, guessed that the Monk was using his imagination. So one day he came alone and extended to the Monk the usual invitation to the village monastery, referring as usual to the ferocious animals of the forest. "Yes, yes, Layman," replied the Monk as before. "Only last night I saw a tiger under yonder tree." "How big was it, my lord?" asked the Mischievous Villager, looking innocent. "It must have been between seven and nine cubits in length," replied the Monk. The Mischievous Villager burst out laughing and said, "My lord, my lord, obviously you have never seen a tiger. No tiger can be bigger than the breadth of my lord's palm. So, sir, be careful next time when you are describing the tiger." The Monk thanked the Mischievous Villager and promised to be more careful in the future.

A few days afterwards a group of villagers arrived and they again invited the Monk to their monastery in the village, mentioning the danger from wild animals. "Yes, yes, Laymen," replied the Monk. "Only last night I saw a tiger under yonder tree and it was as big as my palm." The villagers looked at him in silence and shook their heads. "What is the matter, Laymen?" the Monk asked feebly. "What is wrong with my tiger?" "My lord," the villagers replied, "the average length of a tiger is from seven to nine cubits." "My tiger was all right, my tiger was all right," wailed the Monk, "but that Mischievous Villager dwindled it."

20. When Will the Monk Return?

Prologue: The good lady who offered alms food to the Thingazar Sayadaw was excited and fussy, and she asked, "My lord, was the vegetable soup to your lordship's liking? Was the pork curry a little too salty? And the chicken curry, was there too much chili in it?" The Sayadaw did not answer, but the lady was too dense, and went on asking questions. Finally, the Sayadaw replied, "It is not proper for a monk to pass remarks on the alms food that is offered to him, and if he does, he not only breaks a vow, but brings trouble on his head, as in the case of the Monk and the Cabbage Soup."

A Farmer and his Wife had been able to save some money, and with their savings they built a monastery and installed a Monk in it. The Farmer was good-natured, the Wife was fussy, and the Monk was young. One morning the Wife brought some cabbage soup, rice, and curry and when the Monk had eaten the meal, she asked, "My lord, was the cabbage soup nice?" The Monk did not answer, but the Wife persisted in her questioning. At last the Monk, who wanted to please his patroness, replied, "Laywoman, the cabbage soup was very nice indeed, and, in fact, it is my favorite dish." The Wife went home and said to her husband, "Husband, our Monk's favorite dish is cabbage soup and so you must irrigate your cabbage patch so that there is an adequate Supply of the vegetable throughout the whole year." The Farmer did as he was told, and the Wife offered cabbage soup to the Monk every morning until the latter became sick and tired of it. But he consoled himself with the thought that the rainy season was nearly over, and when the rains stopped the cabbage plants would die.

At last the long rainy season was actually over, but, to the consternation of the poor Monk, the cabbage soup continued to come every morning. Unable to contain himself any longer, he asked the Wife, "Laywoman, surely cabbage is now out of season, and yet you seem to have a large supply of it." "There is no need for my lord to worry," replied the Wife with great satisfaction. "My lord will never lack cabbage soup, for our cabbage patch is well irrigated even in the driest months." The Monk brooded over his misfortune and early next day he left the monastery quietly and went to reside at another village. The Farmer and his Wife were heartbroken over the sudden departure of their Monk and wondered where he had gone.

After some months the Farmer and his Wife learned from an itinerant trader that their Monk was now residing in a village some distance away. They were overjoyed at the news, and the Wife sent with the trader the following message to the Monk:

> "I watch the road,
> I shed a tear.
> When will he return,
> Our Monk so dear,
> Our Golden Monk?"

On his next round, the trader brought from the Monk the following message in reply:

> "Watch not the road,
> Waste not your tear.
> There is no return
> Till your patch is clear
> Of Golden Cabbage."

21. The Old Maid Who Waited for Her Lover

Prologue: "My lord," said the headman of an Irrawaddy Delta village with great enthusiasm, "we have built a fine monastery and we are awaiting the arrival of a monk." "Where is the monk from?" asked the Thingazar Sayadaw. "We do not know yet," replied the headman, "for we have not invited anyone in particular." "Do you mean to say that you are waiting for a monk to turn up at your monastery gate?" asked the Sayadaw. "That is so, my lord," replied the headman. "Unintentionally you are encouraging an unscrupulous person to don the yellow robe and take over your monastery," commented the Sayadaw, "and you may meet disappointment as the Old Maid did when she waited for her Lover."

The Maid was nearly thirty years old, and she began to wonder whether she would be able to get a husband at all. Every evening, for years, she had sat in the front room of her house waiting for young men to come and visit her so that she could choose one as her husband. At the beginning she did attract some visitors, but she found no one to her liking, and now no young men ever came to visit her. She realized she was growing old, and she became anxious and desperate. One morning, however, at the market place she noticed that a young man was looking at her with some interest, and she believed that he would pay a visit to her house that very evening. When evening came she took a bath, put on her finest dress, and sat spinning in the front room of her house, with her back to the door, which was left open.

She waited until the cocks crew the first watch, but nobody came. However, she still felt certain that the young man she saw at the market would come. She brought out the family betel box and started to prepare a chew of betel. At that moment she heard the patter of soft footsteps on the garden path. "He is treading softly as he is feeling very shy," she mused, "so I must forsake my maidenly modesty and must take the initiative myself." She heard the soft footsteps come right behind her, and suddenly they stopped. "He is now standing behind me," she said to herself, and her heart beat fast with excitement. Some moments passed, and again she mused, "He is tongue-tied with longing and with love, and I must start the conversation." So she said aloud, "I have been expecting you the whole evening. Do make yourself at home. If you are tired with the long walk, may I offer you this chew of betel?" Without turning, she lifted her hand to pass the betel. She heard an angry snarl and, turning round, she found an old black dog which, finding the door open, had wandered into the house. She drove the dog away, and, after banging shut the door, she went to bed in disappointment and disgust.

22. The Village Which Liked Long Sermons

Prologue: "My lord," remarked the donor of the alms food, "we never get tired of listening to sermons." "In other words," replied the Thingazar Sayadaw, "you want me to give a long sermon after this meal?" "That is so, my lord," said the donor. "As you wish," replied the Sayadaw, "but remember what happened to the Village which liked to listen to Long Sermons."

There was once a village near Monywa Town in Upper Burma, whose inhabitants never tired of listening to sermons. They had built a fine monastery, but it remained empty most of the time because the residing monks had run away. Those monks who could not give long sermons were not offered alms food, so that they had to run away, and those monks who gave long sermons sooner or later felt the strain, and they too had to run away so as to preserve their life and health. Finally, the village came to be known as the Village Which Liked Long Sermons, and acquired an evil reputation among monks.

After the monastery had remained without a residing monk for three lents in succession, a stout and hefty monk arrived and was installed as the Abbot.

As it was only the tenth day of the waxing moon, the village elders had enough time to get better acquainted with their new Abbot before his first sermon, due to be given on the full-moon day. They were pleased to find the new monk very learned, but they were appalled by the enormous amount of alms food consumed by him every morning. But the Abbot cheerfully explained, "The more I eat, the stronger I become, and the stronger I am, the longer is my sermon."

The day of the full moon arrived, and by noon all the villagers, men, women, and children, assembled in the preaching hall. The Abbot then began his sermon. He preached for two full hours, and the whole congregation remained alert and interested. He preached for another two hours, but by that time the women and the children had become exhausted with listening, and one by one they slipped away. Another two hours elapsed and the sun was setting, but the Abbot showed no sign of stopping. One by one the men slipped away until only the Headman, who sat in the forefront of the congregation, was left. The Abbot went on preaching until the cocks crew their first watch. The Headman was now very tired, and slowly he crawled backwards towards the doorway, but, to his chagrin, he noticed that the Abbot was advancing slowly, keeping pace with him. The Headman reached the door, and continued to crawl backwards. The Abbot followed and went on preaching. Becoming desperate, the Headman stood up, turned round, and ran. But unfortunately, in spite of the full moonlight, he failed to notice an open well near the monastery gate and fell into it.

Fortunately, the well was not deep and the Headman was neither drowned nor injured. But the walls of the well were steep and he found it impossible to climb up by himself, As he stood there, half immersed in water, he saw the Abbot standing above, continuing his sermon. Another hour elapsed and at last the Abbot, taking pity on the shivering layman, said, "You cannot run away now. Shall I go on preaching until dawn when the Sabbath will end?" "My lord," the Headman replied feebly,

"I can say on behalf of the village that it no longer likes long sermons."

23. The Novice Who Mutinied against His Abbot

Prologue: A merchant of Rangoon, who was also a trustee of the Shwedagon Pagoda, said to the Thingazar Sayadaw, "My lord, I do not consider it improper that my lord and the Okpo Sayadaw should be engaged in controversy, for even during the lifetime of the Buddha many learned monks quarreled and argued among themselves." "Layman," replied the Sayadaw with a frown, "you must know that as the drums play, so dance the dancers, and remember the case of the Novice who mutinied against his Abbot."

A man of some fifty years came to a monastery and begged the Abbot to admit him into the order. "I have no family and I have no dependents," he explained. "I am tired of the world and I will forsake it." "But you are too old to change your habits," argued the Abbot, "and I am afraid you will find monastic discipline irksome." "In that case, my lord," the man pleaded, "please admit me as a mere novice and I shall be more than satisfied." Out of pity the Abbot gave him the first ordination and made him a novice. The Novice, in spite of the Abbot's misgivings, proved to be an enthusiastic student of the scriptures and amenable to discipline. He felt so grateful to the Abbot that he became the latter's most ardent admirer and most obedient follower.

One day the old Novice was visited by a group of laymen and laywomen, who whispered to each other, "Let us kneel down and worship this monk of piety and learning. He must have spent his entire lifetime as a monk, and he must be really learned." "No, no, Laypeople," the Novice protested, "I was ordained only recently, and I am still a novice. I have just begun my study of the scriptures and I know very little as yet." Feeling shy and embarrassed, he went and sat down in another part of the monastery. The laymen and laywomen followed him and again whispered to each other:

"How modest, how pious! If he was ordained only recently, obviously he must have been a successful man of affairs who gave up his family and his wealth to lead a life of purity." "Oh, no, no, Laypeople," the Novice explained. "I was merely a farm laborer and I had no family at all." Then he went away hastily to another part of the monastery.

The laymen and laywomen persisted in their admiration of the Novice and, following him, whispered to each other, "Look at his muscles and look at the charms tattooed on his chest and arms. He must have been a mighty man of valor, and surely he has renounced the world after performing great feats of arms. In any case, he must be invulnerable, and no sword or spear can wound him. Even if he bangs his head against the wall, the wall will break but not his skull." This time the Novice was overcome by their flattery, and just to please his admiring audience of laymen and laywomen he banged his head on the wall three or four times, until the Abbot shouted from above the stairs, "What is the matter with you, Novice? My monastery is old and its walls are no longer sound. Stop banging against the wall!" The Novice was taken aback and felt ashamed of himself. But the laymen and laywomen whispered to each other, "Did we not say so? The wall will break but not his head." Encouraged by these whispers, he went on banging the wall with his head. The Abbot shouted, "You dare to disobey me, Novice, you dare to mutiny against my authority? I will disrobe you, I will expel you." The Novice, trembling with fear, paused to look askance at his admiring audience, who clapped their hands and again whispered, "A few more bangs and the wall will crack." At this further encouragement, the Novice, overcoming his awe and fear of the Abbot, went on banging his head over and over again.

24. The Two Monks Who Fought

Prologue: The people of a village near Moulmein had built two monasteries, and on their request two monks were deputed by the Thingazar Sayadaw to reside in them. A few months later some elders of the village came and told the Sayadaw, "My lord, the two monks are doing well indeed. Already the villagers are divided into two groups, one claiming that the monk in the eastern monastery is the better preacher of the two, and the other group maintaining that the monk in the southern monastery is the better preacher." "This is not good news by any means, the Sayadaw commented. "Unless the villagers promise to stop arguing who is the better preacher, I will have to recall my monks. When you get back to the village, please repeat the following tale of the Two Monks Who Fought."There once lived in a monastery two learned and venerable Monks, who used to be famous sculptors in their lay life. One had worked in stone and the other had worked in wood, but since they had entered the order some twenty years before, they had devoted their entire time to studying the scriptures and performing meditative exercises.

The Abbot of the monastery was approaching his eightieth birthday and the villagers had collected from among themselves a substantial sum of money to build a pagoda in the courtyard of the monastery, to be consecrated on the Abbot's birthday. The pagoda was completed some three or four weeks before the auspicious day, but the villagers were disappointed to find that their funds had become exhausted and there was no money left to engage a sculptor to make an image of the Buddha for the newly built pagoda. Then someone remembered that there were two sculptors among the Monks residing in the monastery, and the villagers respectfully requested the two Monks to come to their assistance. "My lords:' they said, "we need only one image, but we cannot decide whether it should be in stone or in wood. So please make one image each, in the material with which your lordships are skillful, and we will choose."

The two Monks, after obtaining the permission of the Abbot, started to chisel and carve, and the villagers anxiously watched. After two or three days, the images began to take shape, and the villagers started to argue which was better, the image in stone or the image in wood. Some more days passed, and the villagers became divided into two groups, one preferring the stone image and the other preferring the wooden one. The spirit of rivalry between the two groups of villagers now infected the two Monks, and, casting jealous glances at each other, they worked feverishly on their images. The auspicious day dawned, and the two images were at last completed. Both proved to be wonderful works of art. But the two groups of villagers continued to argue and dispute, until they came to blows. Seeing their supporters quarreling and fighting, the two Monks also started to fight. At first they hit each other with their fists, but as their anger increased, they hit each other with their images, finally breaking each other's skulls, and also both the images.

25. The Eavesdropper

Prologue: An indignant layman said to the Thingazar Sayadaw, "My lord, the monks in a monastery just outside the city of Moulmein spend their evenings discussing the appearances, love affairs, and intrigues of the laywomen round about the monastery. How I wish there were an Ecclesiastical Censor under the British government, so that appropriate action would be taken against the wayward monks." "Did you actually hear them talking about the laywomen?" asked the Sayadaw. "I certainly did," replied the indignant layman. "Are you a lay brother and therefore a resident of the monastery?" inquired the Sayadaw. "No, my lord," explained the indignant layman, "but every evening after the cocks have crowed their first watch, I climb over the monastery fence, and, crouching near the windows, I listen to the conversation of the monks." "It is wrong of the monks to engage in idle conversation about laywomen," commented the Sayadaw, "but it is equally wrong of you to eavesdrop. If you continue in your nocturnal visits to the monastery, you may find yourself listening to the monks discussing the women of your own household."

It was a Sabbath day, and the Monastery-Donor and his Wife, along with many others, were keeping the Sabbath at the monastery. Since the hour of noon the monks had been meditating and the laymen and laywomen had been telling their beads silently. The sun was now setting and, one by one, the Sabbath-keepers walked out of the monastery slowly and quietly, leaving only the Monastery-Donor and his Wife sitting peacefully in the cool of the monastery garden.

After some moments, and when darkness had fallen, the Wife said, "Let us now go home as it is getting late." Even as she spoke, lights began to twinkle in the various rooms of the monastery. "The great monks have risen from their meditation," replied the Monastery-Donor. "Surely, they will now sit together and discuss some profound point from the scriptures. So let us stay a while and listen to their discussion.

Soon the Monastery-Donor and his Wife heard the monks speaking to each other. "I find the Sabbath day tiring," said one monk, "because on such days I have to be on my best behavior before all the lay people who have come to the monastery to keep their Sabbath." "I find the day interesting," commented another monk. "I notice some very pretty girls among the Sabbath-keepers." "Be careful, be careful," warned the Abbot. "We may be overheard. Are you sure the Sabbath-keepers have gone?" "They have, my lord," a third monk assured him, "and so we can go on with our conversation." "By the way, my lord," said a fourth monk, "I am sure that the tall girl from the big house in the western quarter of the village is having an affair with the village headman's son. I must say, she is quite an attractive young woman." "Her complexion is too dark for my liking," commented a fifth monk. "The daughter of the merchant in the northern quarter has a very fair skin," said the first monk. "But her features are unattractive," remarked the second monk. "In fact, her mother, the merchant's wife, is much prettier than she." "Some matrons can be very alluring," agreed the fourth monk. "Take, for example, the wife of the physician from the southern quarter. Admittedly, she is a little stout, but she still looks youthful and fresh." The Monastery-Donor suddenly jumped up and, pulling his Wife by the hand, rushed out of the monastery gates. "Why are you in such a hurry?" panted the Wife, "The monks' conversation was getting very dangerous for us," explained the Monastery-Donor. "They have finished discussing the pretty women of the northern, southern, and western quarters, and they will soon reach the eastern quarter, and that is where you live."

26. The Old Widow and the Thief

Prologue: During one of his sojourns in Lower Burma the Thingazar Sayadaw made a pilgrimage to the famous Kyaikhtiyo pagoda in Thaton district. As he and his retinue rested at the foot of a hilly slope, a crowd of villagers assembled to pay their respects to the great monk. A young monk passed by and some of the villagers said, "My lord, this monk lives in one of the valleys nearby, and although he has never preached any sermon, he seems to be very learned and pious. People from nearby villages go to his hut-monastery regularly and offer him alms food and robes." "Please go and invite him to come here and meet me," the Sayadaw requested. So one of the villagers ran after the young monk and informed him that the great monk, the Thingazar Sayadaw, wished to see him. The young monk, however, pretended not to hear. The villager repeated the message many times, but the young monk quickened his pace and disappeared down the valley. The villagers were embarrassed, but they insisted, "In spite of his refusal to come before my lord, we are sure that he is a good monk." "Good laymen," replied the Sayadaw, "like the Old Widow, I can only hope that he is good."

The Old Widow had sold her small harvest of paddy at sundown, and so she had no time to take the money to the village headman for safe custody or to call in one of her neighbors to come and stay in the house for the night. At first she was not nervous, but when the cocks crew their first watch and dogs began their barking, she became frightened. Getting up from bed, she sat by the window and looked out into the darkness. The barking of the dogs became more and more furious, and she heard the sound of approaching footsteps. "Who is there?" she shouted out, but there was no answer. She lit the torch which was ready in her hand and raised it across the window. "Who is there?" she called out again. "Only a good man," came the answer from the darkness. "If you are really a good man," suggested the Widow, "you should come into the torchlight." "I am a good man, but I cannot come into the torchlight," replied the intruder. "Come into the torchlight so that I can recognize you," ordered the Old Widow. "I am a good man," insisted the man from the darkness, "but now I am going away." The Old Widow waited until the sound of the footsteps of the intruder faded in the distance and the dogs ceased to bark. Then she sighed to herself, "I can only hope that he was a good man."

27. A Question of Seniority

Prologue: A monk who had recently come to the monastery was causing distress and discontent among the other monks. He was some fifty years old but had spent just one year in the order. He had been an official of the British government, and he found it impossible to forget either his age or his previous rank in lay society. He treated with contempt monks who, although much younger in age, were senior to him by virtue of more years spent as members of the order. At last the abbot of the monastery requested the Thingazar Sayadaw to instruct the wayward monk to mend his ways. Accordingly, the Sayadaw called the monk before him and gave a sermon on the particular rules of canon law pertaining to seniority, humility, and discipline. "But, my lord," protested the monk, "I am much older than the other monks." The Thingazar Sayadaw smiled and said, "Are you insisting that there should be a special method of reckoning to fit your case? Surely you would not like to be placed in the same category as Mistress Sugar from Chindwin Valley."

Mistress Sugar, who lived in a village on the Chindwin River, was a very shrewd business woman, but she was very arrogant. She wanted to have a finger in every pie and she imagined that she knew everything a petty merchant should know. Although forty years of age, she was still a spinster. When some merchants from neighboring villages planned to face the perils of the long river journey and sail down to Rangoon, she decided to accompany them. Arriving at Rangoon, she was able to sell in a short time the merchandise she had brought with her and to make a substantial profit. With the money realized she bought a stall in the vegetable market, which had been set up only a few days before her arrival.

Her business acumen and her forceful personality soon made Mistress Sugar one of the leading stallholders. After some weeks the authorities wanted to appoint an official to superintend the vegetable market, and Mistress Sugar found herself one of the three contenders for the office. Mistress Sugar looked at her two rivals, and came to the conclusion that they were younger than she. She did not take into consideration that people in Rangoon, eating their nutritious rice and living in a milder climate, looked younger than their age. So she suggested that the most senior in years among the three should be chosen to serve as superintendent.

Mistress Sugar's suggestion was accepted, and the three contenders produced their horoscopes. It was found that Mistress Sugar was born in the year 1840, her first rival in the year 1838, and her second rival in the year

1837. But Mistress Sugar was by no means nonplused. "I must be chosen," she said sweetly, "because I am the most senior in years." "You are not," protested her two rivals in anger, "because you are younger than we." "I am the senior," insisted Mistress Sugar, "because my birth year is bigger than yours. That is the way we reckon seniority in the Chindwin Valley."

28. Soft Music Is Better than Medicine

Prologue: A visitor from a nearby village said to the Thingazar Sayadaw, "My lord, in my village there dwells a monk who is very short-tempered and at the same time very miserly. He will not share the alms food that he gets every day with the other monks of the monastery. However, with me he is always patient, and to me he is always generous." "You must be a very tactful person," the Sayadaw replied. "Tact can cure many ills and overcome many difficulties. With an irritable patient, soft music is sometimes better than any medicine."

The Rich Man of the Village was a very short-tempered person to begin with, and, now that he was confined to his bed with a fever, he was irritable and annoyed. The best physicians were called to his bedside, but he found fault with every one of them. He complained that one physician spoke too loudly, another walked with heavy steps, the third one handled him too roughly, and so on. He dismissed every physician with these words, "Here is your fee. Take it, and get out of my sight." There came a time when no more physicians were available and the Rich Man groaned and raved in his bed.

After many weeks, a young Physician from the golden city of Mandalay happened to pass the village on a pilgrimage to a nearby pagoda, and he was approached by the servants of the Rich Man to come and treat their sick master. He was reluctant at first, and the servants pleaded, "Young Physician, we admit that our master is an angry old man and we must confess that he has insulted and dismissed all the physicians of the neighborhood. But he is really sick, and perhaps your courteous manners and pleasant personality will soothe our master."

The Physician, taking his cue from the remarks made by the servants, entered the sickroom very softly and very gently. Then he whispered into the Rich Man's ear, "Oh, my poor Uncle, how are you feeling today?" He signed to one of the servants to come near him and softly asked for some perfumed water. When the perfumed water had been brought, he rinsed his hands with it. Then he lightly felt the fevered brow of the Rich Man and asked, "Esteemed Uncle, will you please honor me by drinking the medicine which I am going to prepare for you now?" The Rich Man nodded, and the young Physician quietly mixed his medicine, and at the same time he sang softly as follows:

"Sweet medicine for sweet Uncle,
  Gentle medicine for gentle Uncle;
  Please just take one dose,
  And Uncle shall be well forever."

The Rich Man was soothed by the song, and after drinking the medicine he fell asleep. He slept as soundly as a child the whole night, and the following morning, when he woke up, he found that his fever had gone and he was fit and well again.

29. The Widow Who Lost Her Silver Coins

Prologue: The Thingazar Sayadaw, noticing that a newly ordained monk was not present at the evening assembly, inquired why he was absent. "My lord," replied one of the assembled monks, "he has been upset by the theft of his whole set of robes, and begs to be excused." The Sayadaw immediately sent for the monk, and, when he arrived said, "Only this afternoon I received a full set of robes as an offering, and I will give it to you after the assembly. But please do not behave like the old Widow who lost her entire savings consisting of five silver coins.

Once there lived in a village an old Widow. She had no children, and was very poor, but in spite of her extreme poverty she was very pious. Every evening she could be seen by the light of a votive oil lamp, kneeling before the altar in the front room of her little cottage. As the evening advanced, her voice, reciting the scriptures and telling her beads, was heard by the neighbors. As the cocks crew the first watch of the night, her words of prayer, "May all beings be well and happy, and may they take a share in my deeds of merit," echoed all over the village.

One night no votive light was seen, and darkness and silence enveloped the little cottage. The neighbors waited for some time and then went and knocked at the door, asking with anxiety, "Mother, is everything all right with you?" "I am all right," replied the Widow from inside. The neighbors, out of politeness, did not ask any more questions, although they were puzzled as to why the Widow was not saying her usual evening prayers. Four or five evenings passed, but still the votive light was not seen and no prayers were heard from the Widow's cottage. The villagers could not bear the mystery any longer, and bluntly said to the Widow, "We have become so used to seeing the votive light in your cottage and hearing your prayers that we feel distressed and are puzzled as to why you have suddenly ceased to be pious." The Widow sighed softly and replied, "My Sons, my Daughters, through hard work and thrift I had been able to save five silver coins, but some days ago, when I was away at work, some headless thief broke into my cottage and stole my precious silver coins. I am heartbroken over the loss, and I find that I cannot say my prayers." The villagers were relieved to get the explanation, and in no time they collected from among themselves five silver coins and gave them to the Widow.

The next evening the villagers quietly assembled in front of the little cottage, full of joy and expectation, but, to their great disappointment, they saw no votive light and heard no sound of prayers. They waited till the first watch was over and then went and knocked at the door. "Mother, Mother," they shouted, "you now have five silver coins, and yet you are not reciting your scriptures!" "Sons and Daughters," came the reply, "it is true that, through your kindness, I have five silver coins. Still I cannot pray, because my mind keeps brooding on the fact that, if there had been no theft, there would have been ten silver coins."

30. Mistress Monastery-Donor Who Broke into a Dance

Prologue: The good lady was full of enthusiasm and admiration for one of the monks among the Thingazar Sayadaw's retinue. "My lord," she said, "the young monk who gave the sermon at yesterday's alms-giving in the town was simply wonderful. His voice was clear, yet sweet to the ear, and he was indeed a master of words. He preached for one whole hour, and yet his voice never faltered, but remained clear and musical." The Sayadaw smiled and remarked, "I hope you did not get up and dance as the Monastery-Donor did in the village of Lone Palm Tree."

In the village of Lone Palm Tree there lived a Widow who had built and donated five monasteries in memory of her late husband. She had installed an abbot in each monastery, but she was dissatisfied with them all, because she found their sermons dull and uninteresting. Each Sabbath day she held a great almsgiving ceremony, at the conclusion of which one of the abbots was invited to give a sermon. With tears in her eyes, as she thought of her husband, she knelt before the assembled monks and listened ardently to the sermon. But always at the end she commented, "A poor sermon indeed. I despair of ever hearing a good sermon before I die." The abbots felt distressed at her remarks. They read and reread their scriptures. They practiced till their voices became hoarse. They tried and tried. But when the Sabbath day came round again the Monastery-Donor, the pious Widow, remained as dissatisfied with their sermons as before. One evening a troupe of strolling players arrived at the village and took shelter for the night in the village rest-house. Some villagers dropped in to greet the players, and in the course of their conversation they mentioned that, although there were five abbots in the village, not one among them could give sermons to the Monastery-Donor satisfactorily. One of the clowns in the troupe inquired, "Are they not learned? Know they not their scriptures?" "They are learned and they know their scriptures," explained the villagers. "The fault is in the tone and in the style of delivery." Later in the evening the Clown became drunk with toddy wine and wandered into one of the monasteries. Going straight to the Abbot, he whispered, "My lord, you should sing your sermon to this tune: 'Tra La La La La, Tra La Ia La La.' The tune, my lord, is the dance tune of our troupe and is very popular with all audiences."

The following Sabbath day it happened that the particular Abbot to whom the Clown had taught the dance tune was chosen to give the sermon. At first he used his usual tone and style, but he became desperate when he noticed the Monastery-Donor shaking her head in disappointment and dissatisfaction. So he sang out his words to the dance tune. The other abbots were startled and the kneeling villagers looked up in horror, but a happy smile slowly appeared on the Monastery-Donor's face. Thus encouraged, the Abbot went on singing out his sermon until the Monastery-Donor, in great ecstasy, stood up and danced.

31. One Prescription Is Enough

Prologue: A monk from a village some miles away from Moulmein came and paid respect to the Thingazar Sayadaw. "My lord," he said, "I must confess that I have not studied the scriptures, and I only know one single *Jataka*, namely, that of the Wise Hare, who offered his own body as alms food for a mendicant. Still, using this one Birth Story, I have been giving sermons to my villagers for the last three years. The Sayadaw was surprised and asked, "The particular *Jataka* you mentioned seems suitable for occasions like an initiation or an almsgiving, but on other occasions, for example, a funeral, how do you manage?" "The same *Jataka* has to serve all kinds of occasions, my lord," replied the monk. "You are indeed fortunate," the Sayadaw commented with a smile, "as fortunate as Physician Extraordinary and his one Prescription."

During the early days of the Kingdom of Ava a stranger from the Yaw Valley near the Chin Hills passed through the city on a pilgrimage, and was given shelter for the night by a poor Farmer and his Wife at their house on the outskirts of Ava. During the night the Farmer, whose name happened to be "Master Extraordinary," had an attack of colic, and was nursed and comforted by his Wife. Their guest for the night inquired what was troubling the Farmer and the Wife replied, "For seven long years my husband has been suffering from colic, and no physician has been able to cure him." The guest, after examining the patient, said, "I happen to be a master of magic, witchcraft, and physic, and for your hospitality I will give you my prescription for colic. Mix thoroughly one tical of ripe tamarind fruit, one tical of salt, and one tical of soda, and take one teaspoonful of the mixture the last thing at night." In the morning the stranger left to continue his pilgrimage, and the Wife prepared the medicine as prescribed and gave the required dose to her husband. As the medicine was really a strong purgative, Master Extraordinary was cured of his colic within two or three days.

The Governor of the city was also a sufferer from colic, and, after a very painful attack, he sent criers all over the city to proclaim a reward of one thousand silver coins to the physician who could cure his colic. Master Extraordinary heard the proclamation and, goaded on by his Wife, pretended to be a physician, and, going to the bedside of the Governor, offered to cure him of his malady. That night he gave a spoonful of his own medicine to the Governor, who, after a good purging, found himself cured. Master Extraordinary not only received the promised reward but also became famous as a great physician. Hundreds of patients suffering from various kinds of diseases came to him for treatment. At first he wanted to confess that he was not a physician, but his Wife pointed out to him that he would certainly be executed by the Governor if the truth should become known. In desperation Master Extraordinary shared his medicine with all the patients. Fortunately for him, a good purging always had salutary effects on all, and Master Extraordinary came to be known as "Physician Extraordinary."

One day the only daughter of the King became afflicted with sore eyes. Physician Extraordinary was at once sent for, and he had no choice but to give a spoonful of his medicine to the lovely Princess. The whole of that night Physician Extraordinary and his Wife lay awake, because they were certain his fraud would be discovered and he would be executed the following day. When morning came, however, it was found that, after a good purging, the eyes of the Princess were clear and bright again, and Physician Extraordinary became even more famous.

One evening two bullock-cart men came to consult Physician Extraordinary. They were simple villagers who had come to the city with a load of paddy. After delivering their paddy they fell asleep on the roadside, and, when they woke up, they found their bullocks had been stolen. They were now consulting Physician Extraordinary as to the whereabouts of their bullocks, because they thought Extraordinary was a great astrologer. Physician Extraordinary, without further ado, gave a spoonful of his medicine to each and told them to go back to their village. The two cartmen were too timid to say any more and they slept the night on their carts. At the first streak of dawn they started on their homeward journey, leaving their carts behind. After they had walked for about a mile the medicine took effect, and they had to leave the road and go behind some bushes to ease themselves. But the bushes happened to be the very bushes in which the thieves had hidden their bullocks. So the cartmen went back to their carts in great joy, riding on their bullocks. When they arrived back at Ava they told their story in the market place. Thus Physician Extraordinary won added fame as a great astrologer.

32. How Master Lazybones Obtained a Wife

Prologue: One of the young monks from a monastery in a town in Middle Burma became tired of monastic life. With the permission of the abbot, he left the order and became a layman again. Some months later he came back to the monastery. Several monks who used to be his companions made fun of him and asked, "How are you getting on?" "Sirs, I am now married," replied the young layman. "Bravo!" said the monks. "But how did you manage that?" "A dog helped me," replied the young layman. "I fell in love with a young woman, but her parents did not like me, and locked the gates so that I could not enter and plead with the young woman to marry me. However, I saw a dog enter the back garden through a hole in the fence. I followed him, knocked at the door of the house, and thus was able to see my beloved." The Thingazar Sayadaw, who was on a visit to the monastery, overheard him and commented, "Young Layman, you remind me of how Master Lazybones obtained a wife through the help of a rat."

(M) aster Lazybones, as his name implied, was very indolent and would not do any work. One day, while taking a stroll near the village pagoda, he saw a rat coming out of a big hole under the wall of the pagoda, carrying a large piece of cake in its mouth. Although unwilling to work, Lazybones was an intelligent young fellow, and he guessed that the animal had come through a tunnel leading to the altar standing in front of the big statue of the Buddha inside the pagoda. Being also inquisitive, he crept into the hole and found the tunnel, which, to his surprise, was big enough for him to get into. He crawled forward for some fifty yards and found himself under the great statue. Then he noticed a small hole big enough only for a rat, obviously leading to the altar. He guessed that the tunnel had been dug by thieves some years before, in troubled times, to carry off the offerings of gold and jewels vaulted underneath the statue, and that the little hole had been made by rats to steal the daily offerings of alms food placed on the altar.

When the next full-moon day came round, Lazybones stood near the hole in the wall and waited for the Wife of the rich Merchant of the village, who regularly brought her offerings of alms food to the pagoda on Sabbath days. When he saw the Merchant's Wife approaching, he jumped into the hole and crawled through the tunnel until he was right underneath the statue. He put his ear against the rathole and listened to the old lady saying her prayers. When she had finished he put his mouth against the hole and said, "For your deed of merit I will reward you with valuable advice. Marry your daughter to a young man called Lazybones, who will become a very rich merchant," In great excitement the old lady told her husband of the advice given by the great statue. "You are a silly woman," the Merchant replied. "How can a statue speak?" "It is you who are silly," the Wife argued. "If you do not believe what I say, go and offer some alms food yourself the next Sabbath day."

The next Sabbath day the old Merchant knelt before the altar, offered alms food, and said his prayers. After the Merchant had concluded his prayers with the usual words, "In this, my deed of merit, may all beings take a share, "Lazybones spoke from underneath the statue, "For your deed of merit, I will reward you with valuable advice. Marry your daughter to a young man called Lazybones, who will become a great merchant." The old Merchant hurried home and conferred with his Wife. Together they said to their Daughter, "Beloved daughter, with the great statue's advice we have found a nice young man for you to marry, and he is no other than Lazybones." The Daughter was rebellious. "I do not love him, nor do I even know him," she protested. "Moreover, I do not believe that the statue really spoke." "Then, Daughter," suggested the Merchant, "you can find out for yourself. Go and offer alms food to the statue,"

The following Sabbath day the Daughter walked towards the pagoda with a tray of alms food on her head. At the gate she found a young man who greeted her with these words: "Lovely maiden, may I carry your tray for you? I have come to the pagoda to worship and pray, and I am indeed fortunate to find you as my companion in merit. My name is Lazybones, but I am not so lazy as my name implies." So the two young people went inside the pagoda, and offered alms food and prayed together. Lazybones confessed to the young girl the trick he had played on her parents. "But you must excuse me," he pleaded, "for I did it all for the love of you." She laughed, and, taking him along with her, she went back to her parents. "Beloved Parents," she announced, "the statue did not say anything, perhaps because Master Lazybones was also present. However, I am an obedient and dutiful daughter and will marry the young man of your choice."

33. Why the Tawny Dog Ran Away

Prologue: Two senior monks residing together in a monastery quarreled and as a result they ceased to speak to each other. The poor lay brother found himself in a very awkward position, for when he attended one monk, the other became jealous. Finally, one day, one of the monks in a jealous rage threw a spittoon at the lay brother's head. The lay brother went and reported the matter to the Thingazar Sayadaw. The Sayadaw called up the two quarreling monks and said, "It is childish and undignified for monks to quarrel, it is stupid and silly for monks not to be on speaking terms. Moreover, good lay brothers are rarer than gold, and, if you vent your tempers on the poor fellow, he will soon run away as the Tawny Dog did."

Master Round Gold and his wife Mistress Glass found a tawny puppy wandering in the streets and took him home. As no owner turned up to claim him, he became their pet. As years passed he grew into a fine watchdog, and became well known in the village as the "Tawny Dog."

The marriage was a happy one until Master Round Gold took to drinking toddy wine occasionally. On those evenings when he came home drunk he always greeted his wife Mistress Glass with a loud demand to be served dinner immediately, and always Mistress Glass took offense and refused to serve the dinner. In their anger Master Round Gold would give a kick to the poor Tawny Dog and Mistress Glass would strike the poor animal with her ladle. Soon the Tawny Dog learned to slink out of the house and disappear for the night whenever he heard his master demanding to be served dinner. Master

Round Gold became more and more addicted to toddy wine, and became a real drunkard. Instead of drinking occasionally, he drank every day, with the result that he came home drunk every evening. The Tawny Dog, realizing that he would be kicked and beaten every night, ran away and became pet and watchdog at the house of the village Headman.

34. The Abbot Who Missed His Lay Brother

Prologue: One afternoon, just as the Thingazar Sayadaw was beginning his lecture to a class of junior monks, an invitation was received by the monastery to send a monk to conduct a funeral service in the town. The lecture was for the junior monks, but the senior monks, being scholars, wanted to attend it. So a newly ordained monk, some fifty years of age, was deputed to go. Although he looked venerable because of his age, he was not learned at all and therefore was barely able to give the Five Precepts. He was reluctant to go, but the monks pointed out to him that at a funeral service a monk was rarely called upon to give a sermon. The newly ordained monk duly went, but he was so excited that he forgot to say the exhortation after giving the Five Precepts. To make matters worse, he was asked by the bereaved family to give a sermon. With a red face, he confessed that he could not give one. When he returned to the monastery, he informed the monks of his discomfiture at the funeral. The Thingazar Sayadaw, overhearing him, said, "You should have shouted, 'I miss my lay brother, I miss my lay brother,' as Monk Flying Palm Leaves did at a village in Upper Burma."

In a village in Upper Burma there once lived an Abbot who was affectionately called by his followers "Monk Flying Palm Leaves." He was a great preacher, and his sermons were praised and acclaimed by all. But in actual fact he was an ignoramus, and all his sermons were written by his faithful Lay Brother, "Full Shine" by name. The Abbot, to give him his due, matched the Lay Brother's learning with his industry, and after the Lay Brother had written a sermon the Abbot would spend a whole night learning it by heart. Everything went smoothly for many years, until a death by accident occurred in the village. As, according to the custom, the victim of an accident had to be buried before nightfall, the announcement of the funeral was made immediately, and the Abbot was invited without notice to conduct the funeral service. The result was that the Lay Brother had no time to compose a sermon suitable to the occasion. The Abbot, however, was not unduly worried, for at a funeral a monk was rarely asked to give a sermon.

But the Abbot, in thinking that he would not be called upon to give a sermon, forgot to take into consideration his reputation as a champion sermon-giver. After he had given the Five Precepts, the bereaved Widow said, "My lord, our hearts are broken over this sudden loss; therefore, may we have a sermon which will lighten our burden of sorrow?" The Abbot, however, remained silent. After some moments the Widow could no longer restrain her grief, and, breaking into sobs, cried out in anguish, "How I miss my husband! How I miss my husband!" The Abbot also broke into sobs and cried out in anguish, "How I miss my Lay Brother Full Shine! How I miss my Lay Brother Full Shine!"

35. Monk Lily Tray from East Rangoon

Prologue: Once, when the Sayadaw was keeping lent in a monastery in Moulmein, a company of young monks from a town some fifty miles away came to pay their respects to him. The learned monk preached a special sermon which was greatly appreciated by the visitors. Then the Sayadaw asked them, "Are you not keeping lent at your place? If so, by coming to Moulmein, you are breaking your vow to keep lent." "But, my lord," the young monks argued, "surely our canon law permits us, in an emergency, to leave our monastery where we are keeping lent?" "Pray, what is the emergency?" asked the Sayadaw. "The emergency is our great desire to come and worship and listen to my lord's sermons," explained one of the young monks. The Sayadaw smiled and said, "I only trust that you will not prove yourselves to be ardent pupils of Monk Lily Tray from East Rangoon."

In the new capital of Rangoon there lived a very famous and popular monk by the name of Reverend Lily Tray. He was given that name by his many followers because his face was always bright and beaming, like a bunch of lilies on a well-polished tray of brass. He resided in a wonderful monastery in the eastern part of the city, built especially for him by the rich merchants of East Rangoon. A tireless traveler, he frequently visited Pegu, Bassein, Prome, and other Lower Burmese towns, which made him very popular also with the rich merchants of those places. In fact, he specialized in rich merchants, and always interpreted the scriptures in such a way as to accommodate and soothe their consciences.

One year, however, when he visited Prome, some one hundred and fifty miles north of Rangoon, a Rich Merchant of that town was quite distressed, because it was during the three months' period of lent, and obviously Monk Lily Tray had broken his vow. So he expressed his sorrow and distress that such a famous monk should set an evil example to young monks by breaking lent. Monk Lily Tray, smiling broadly, replied, "Layman, you do not understand. I have not broken lent." The Merchant argued, "My lord, surely you recited the formula of keeping lent, containing these words: 'I undertake to keep the three months of the coming lent within the precincts of this particular monastery!'" "Of course, I did," retorted Monk Lily Tray, with some show of anger. There was a pause, during which Monk Lily Tray collected his thoughts and recovered his composure. Beaming brightly again, he said, "Of course, I had to change the formula a little. I substituted 'universe' for 'monastery,' and remember, layman, Prome and East Rangoon are within this particular universe."

36. The Monk Who Became an Oil-Vendor

Prologue: The abbot of a monastery in Rangoon invited the Thingazar Sayadaw to give an address to his junior monks, exhorting them to be pious and pure, and warning them against the temptation to return to lay life on expectation of fame and wealth. In the opinion of the abbot such exhortations and warnings were absolutely necessary in view of the fact that scores of monks had doffed their robes in the hope that they would become rich and famous as physicians, astrologers, or government officials. The Thingazar Sayadaw, in giving his address, pointed out that, in spite of many social and political changes in the country, monks still retained the respect and the regard of the people, and monks worthy of the name should follow as before the path of purity and learning. "Monks," concluded the Sayadaw, "do not think that you with your classical learning can compete with those young men educated in the new lay schools for appointments as government servants. And do not believe that the present popularity of native medicine and astrology can last long. You have been novices and monks for some years now, and, should you re-embrace the lay life, you will find yourselves out of touch and out of place. It is certain that you will find yourselves in trouble, like the Monk who became an Oil-Vendor."

A middle-aged monk, living in a village not far from the town of Pakokku, suddenly found monastic life irksome, and, after obtaining the necessary permission from his abbot, he became a layman again. At first his monastic learning won him some respect, and, by using his knowledge of classical music, literature, medicine, and astrology, he was able to eke out a living, He married a girl from among his circle of admirers, but, with the passing of time, his novelty and popularity waned, and people no longer consulted him on the subjects of his past studies. The admiring girl and pupil also changed into a shrew and tyrant. One morning she scolded, "You good-for-nothing Former-Monk, why did you marry a wife knowing that you could not earn a living? You do not know how to plow or sow or reap. You do not know any craft."

The hinterland of Pakokku had always been a sesame oil producing region, and the Former-Monk decided that at least he could earn a living as a vendor of oil. However, as he had been a monk for such a long time, he found it difficult to discard his dignified mien. "What a conceited-looking old fellow!" people murmured when they saw him at the market. In addition, he was shy and gentle, and could not shout out the excellence of his ware, as ordinary oil-vendors did in their vulgar way. Above all, he could not tell a lie, and while other oil-vendors cried out, "We are reducing our price, we are selling at a loss; yet our oil is absolutely pure," he remained silent. Naturally, his sales were very poor and, after a few days, his Wife scolded again, "Oh, you prince of virtue, you paragon of truthfulness! If you are so pious and pure, why did you marry at all?"

Our Oil-Vendor brooded for many days and finally decided that he would brave the discomfort of storm and rain, and dangers and difficulties at the Anglo-Burmese frontier, and take a cargo of oil down the river to Rangoon. In spite of his lack of experience, his shyness, and his dignified mien, he was able to sell his cargo quickly in the sesame oil-starved city of Rangoon, and he soon found himself with some two hundred rupees. He took passage back to Pakokku, but, unfortunately, just as his boat was approaching the town, it capsized in a gust of wind. Our Oil-Vendor was able to swim ashore, but his bedroll together with his two hundred rupees sewn in the pillow went down with the boat. "Alas, alas," he cried to himself, "how can I return to my village without even my capital of some fifty rupees? My Wife will scold me and no one in my village will believe that I did sell my oil at a huge profit."

Then he had an idea. "People in Pakokku are kind," he mused, "and sesame oil is plentiful here. I have just to go to every house and beg for a small measure of oil as a poor shipwrecked person. Every housewife will give, and very soon I shall have three or four pots full of oil. With the oil so collected, I will go down to Rangoon again and sell it at the usual profit." So he went to the back door of the nearest house and said, "Laywoman, can you offer me some oil?" The housewife looked at him and said, "What do you mean by calling me a laywoman? You are not a monk." The servant maids also looked at him, and, bursting into laughter, they jeered, "Old Former-Monk, you are no longer a monk, and why should we show respect to you?" In shame and in disgust he returned to his village, and, standing before his Wife and tearing his hair, he lamented, "Oh, oh, why did I ever leave the abode of happiness for this region of suffering? But it is now too late for regrets. So, you woman of evil and greed, scold me and abuse me and I will suffer without complaint."

37. Master Extraordinary and the Glutinous Rice

Prologue: While the Thingazar Sayadaw was on a visit to Rangoon he was asked the following question by a layman who had studied the scriptures in some detail: "Why do the commentaries sometimes make statements in direct opposition to statements given in the texts themselves?" The Sayadaw said that he had found no such conflicting statements and requested the layman to give some examples. The layman complied with two or three examples, but they were proved not to be conflicting at all. The Sayadaw explained that the statements appeared to be against the texts only because the layman had not grasped the style of some of the commentaries. "Learned Layman," the Sayadaw said with a smile, "you are like Master Extraordinary and the Glutinous Rice."

The harvest had been gathered and the sowing season was still some weeks away. So Master Extraordinary had no work to do. It was, however, a busy season for his Wife, who was a seller of steamed glutinous rice, a delicacy served at feasts and festivals held in the holiday period before the advent of the monsoon. One day she was faced with a problem. The following morning there was to be a great festival at a pagoda some miles away, and the following night there was to be a public theatrical show in her own village; so she asked herself, "Who will prepare the glutinous rice for the evening function? I cannot be back from the pagoda until late in the afternoon and it takes hours to steam the glutinous rice." Master Extraordinary overheard her words and intervened, "My dear, I know how to sow and how to reap any rice, whether ordinary or glutinous, and surely I should know how to steam it. You women always complain of overwork in the house, but you also think that men are stupid and do not know how to cook. I have nothing to do the whole day, and gladly will I prepare the rice, so that when you come back from the pagoda you will find it ready, hot and steaming." "Husband," protested the Wife, "this is your short period of rest between seasons, and, moreover, preparing glutinous rice needs care and patience." However, she was finally persuaded to agree. So early next morning the Wife, with her basket and trays, proceeded to the pagoda festival.

Master Extraordinary watched the sun carefully so as not to be late, and by midday the pots of glutinous rice were on the fire. He sang and whistled to pass the time, and after about an hour he removed the lids from the pots to have a peep into them. To his surprise and annoyance, he found the rice uncooked. He put in more firewood and waited for some more minutes. He opened the lids and looked again, and to his bewilderment he found the rice still uncooked. He now suspected witchcraft or interference by evil spirits. "That old woman from the corner house," mused Master Extraordinary, "is surely a witch and she has never liked me, or perhaps evil spirits are jealous of these religious festivals and have therefore laid a spell on my rice." Trembling with excitement and anger, and perspiring profusely, he burned more and more firewood but it was of no avail. The Wife returned late in the afternoon and Master Extraordinary, red-faced with shame and anger, greeted her with the words, "Curse the witches, curse the spirits, the rice will not boil." The Wife removed the lids and peered into the pots and then she said sweetly, "Dear husband, you have not put any water in the lower pots."

38. Master Tall and the Buffaloes

Prologue: A merchant of Rangoon, who was also a trustee of the Shwedagon Pagoda, complained before the Thingazar Sayadaw: "The revival of interest in our religion has resulted in a spate of books on the scriptures, but many of them are conflicting, and some of them must be worthless. But I am bewildered; I do not know which of these books should be read and which books should be discarded." "The scriptures themselves are there to guide you," advised the Sayadaw, "and you must learn to select and choose. Do not lose yourself among the books as Master Tall did among the buffaloes."

Master Tall, as his name implied, was a strapping young man of sixteen years, but he possessed no intelligence. He was sent by his father to the monastery, as were other boys by their fathers, but, although he was obedient to the monks and popular with the other lads of the monastery, he learned nothing. It was now time for him to leave the monastery and earn a living, but his father could not get him any employment outside, and he was practically useless on his father's farm. Finally he became a herdsman, caring for his father's three buffaloes. Poor Master Tall found it impossible to distinguish one buffalo from another, and therefore, once he had put his father's buffaloes to pasture, he could not trace them among the buffaloes of other herdsmen. Discovering this failing of Master Tall's, the other herdsmen took advantage of it. They just lay at ease on the grass, playing on their reed pipes or laughing and joking, and whenever they saw a buffalo going astray or wandering onto a piece of farmland, they shouted, "Master Tall, Master Tall, there goes your buffalo!" Master Tall, thinking every buffalo that strayed was his, spent the whole long day chasing and catching the buffaloes. Moreover, when evening came, he had to wait till the other herdsmen had taken away all their buffaloes, leaving behind the three belonging to his father, so that when he arrived home it was late. This happened for many days, until his anxious father made inquiries and found out the trick played on his son.

So the next day the fond father placed wreaths made of toddy-palm leaves on the horns of his three buffaloes, and said, "Now my son, look at the buffaloes carefully and remember that only a buffalo which has a wreath of toddy-palm leaves round his horns is your responsibility. Do not tire yourself by herding all the buffaloes of the village." That morning, whenever the other herdsmen shouted, "Hey, Master Tall, there goes your animal," Master Tall glanced at the straying buffalo's horns, and if he saw no wreath on its horns, he just sat down and took no further notice. However, by midday Master Tall's secret had been discovered by his companions, who promptly put wreaths of toddy-palm leaves on the horns of their buffaloes too, with the result that poor Master Tall spent the entire afternoon chasing all stray buffaloes. He was late again in reaching home, and to his anxious father, who had been waiting for him at the gate of his house, Master Tall complained, "Father, all was well in the morning, but at midday wreaths of toddy-palm leaves sprouted on the horns of the other buffaloes also."

39. The Haughty Ferryman

Prologue: An inhabitant of the small town of Beelin near Moulmein had lately taken up the study of the scriptures and, in his enthusiasm, had become a lay preacher. But his interpretations of the scriptures were unorthodox, and especially in one matter he was adamant. One of the Beatitudes mentioned in the scriptures was the blessing of endowing one's family with valuable gifts. The lay preacher insisted that "valuable gifts" did not refer to gold and silver, cattle and land, but to religious exhortation only. Therefore, he put forward the thesis that it was wrong for a man to procure riches for his family. His listeners refused to accept this interpretation and challenged him to go along with them to the Thingazar Sayadaw at Moulmein. He accepted the challenge and accompanied a delegation of Beelin folks to Moulmein. Arriving at the monastery where the Sayadaw was staying, the visitors from Beelin explained the purpose of their visit. The Sayadaw, after hearing them, asked the lay preacher, "Have the delegates correctly stated the position?" "They have, my lord," replied the lay preacher. "I am afraid your interpretation is wrong," the Sayadaw went on, "but let us discuss it carefully." "There is no need to discuss it, my lord," the lay preacher replied. "If my lord says that it is wrong, it must be wrong." At this surprising answer, the visitors from Beelin burst out laughing and the Sayadaw said, "Friend, you remind me of the Haughty Ferryman of Nyaung-oo."

I n the town of Nyaung-oo, near the ancient ruins of Pagan, there lived a Ferryman, who had an evil reputation among travelers because he was haughty and ill-mannered. He was undoubtedly a very skillful ferryman, and he rowed hundreds of travelers every day across the Irrawaddy river. Although the usual fee for a ferry ride was a quarter, he often demanded and received a full silver coin, because no traveler was courageous enough to protest.

One full-moon day, a Lay Brother from a monastery in one of the villages opposite Nyaung-oo took the ferry, because he wanted to attend a festival at one of the pagodas at Pagan. The Ferryman demanded one silver coin as his fee and the Lay Brother paid without any protest. The Lay Brother enjoyed himself at the festival and visited many amusement booths and many food-stalls, for he was a jolly person and loved good food. Suddenly he noticed that the sun was setting, and, realizing that his abbot would be very cross should he fail to return to the monastery by nightfall, he hurried back to the ferry. The road to the riverside was dusty and full of merry people going to the festival, for plays and puppet shows would give performances throughout the night. The Lay Brother was repeatedly jostled by the crowd and he became angry. By the time he reached the ferry he was indeed in a fiery temper.

As he stepped onto the ferry, the Ferryman said gruffly, "Can you not wait until the morning? It is getting dark." "It is not dark yet and there is plenty of time to row to the other side and back," the Lay Brother replied. "All right," said the Ferryman, "I will row you across for a fee of two silver coins." The Lay Brother felt in his pockets and found that, as he had been on a spending spree at the festival, he had only a quarter piece left. He was now angry as well as desperate, and protested to the Ferryman, "The ferry fee fixed by customary law is only a silver quarter. There is no storm nor any other hazard in the crossing, and I must fight for my rights. Let us wrestle."

So saying, the Lay Brother took up a fighting stance. The Ferryman glanced at the Lay Brother and, noting that he was stout and hefty and in a fighting mood, replied meekly, "Lay Brother, my fee is only half a quarter coin."

40. The Farmer Who Was Afraid of His Wife

Prologue: A young monk gave a sermon to the people of a small town in Lower Burma, and, as he had been studying the scriptures with some diligence, he impressed his listeners so much that some of them flattered him: "My lord is as good a preacher as the Thingazar Sayadaw now residing at Moulmein." Becoming conceited, he boasted, "I am better than the Thingazar. I can question him on many points and, whatever his answers are, I will challenge their correctness." Some mischievous young men of the town took him at his word and offered to escort him to Moulmein. The boastful monk had to agree, and some days later he and the young men reached the monastery where the Sayadaw was staying. The young men explained the purpose of their visit and the Thingazar Sayadaw invited the boastful monk to ask his questions. "My lord," asked the conceited monk, "what is the correct interpretation of this quotation from the scriptures?" The Thingazar Sayadaw, after listening to the quotation, gave his answer. "I am in entire agreement with my lord's interpretation," said the conceited monk, "and I have no more questions to ask." The young men burst out laughing and the Thingazar Sayadaw commented, "Your monk reminds me of the Farmer who was afraid of his Wife."

he young bachelors of the village were in a jolly mood. They put up at the market place posters which read: "A husband who is afraid of his wife is not a man at all, but an animal with a foul smell." A Farmer passing by thought that they were referring to him in particular. So he challenged them to a fight, shouting, "Who says that I am afraid of my wife?" "Restrain your anger, uncle," replied the young men. "We are not accusing anybody, we are merely making a statement." "Then will you admit that I am master in my own house?" asked the Farmer. "We admit nothing," replied the young men, "and we do not believe in hearsay, we believe only our own eyes." "Then come with me to my home," invited the Farmer, "and from the gate you can watch my wife serving me dinner with humility, affection, and respect."

Accordingly, the young men followed him to the gate of his house, and stood there waiting and watching. The Farmer went into the house, and shouting "Wife, I am here," sat down. The Wife came out of the kitchen, laid the table, and started to serve the dinner. Wanting to impress the young men outside, he raised his voice and said, "Wife, the curry is too salty and I cannot eat it." The Wife, with a look of surprise, replied, "I tasted it and it was not salty at all." "Woman," insisted the Farmer, "I tell you the curry is salty." "What ails you, man?" the Wife shouted back in anger. "Since the day I first married you many years ago, you have never complained about my cooking. If you think that the curry is salty, I will throw it to the dogs, and I will never cook your meals any more." Without another word the Farmer ate his dinner, and when he had finished he said, "Sweet wife, when eaten together with the rice the curry did not taste salty at all; in fact it was simply delicious." The young men, overhearing this final remark on the part of the Farmer, clapped their hands and went away.

41. The Townsman Who Pitied the Blacksmith

Prologue: Two lay preachers disputed the interpretation of some sentences from the scriptures and took the matter to the Thingazar Sayadaw for his decision. The Sayadaw pointed out that both the lay preachers were incorrect in their interpretations and gave the correct interpretation. "I am not so stupid, my lord," said the first lay preacher, "but I was misled by my dictionary." "I am not so stupid either," the second lay preacher joined in, "but I was misled by my grammar book." "Lay preachers," the Sayadaw advised, "do not blame the dictionary and the grammar book. If you do, you will be reminding people of the foolish Townsman who pitied the Blacksmith."

A Townsman was paying a visit to his relations in a village. He wanted to join his relations in their various chores, but found himself unskillful and inexperienced. As a desperate measure, he offered to cut down a tree for firewood. "Unfortunately, we broke our ax the other day," replied his hosts. Saying, "I will go and buy another," the Townsman went to the village smithy and saw a dozen pickaxes on display. Not knowing the difference between an ax and a pickax, he did not ask for an ax, but bought one of the displayed pickaxes. Returning to the house of his relations, he endeavored to cut down the tree with the pickax but without success.

His relations came out to watch him cut down the tree, and they burst out laughing when they saw him using the pickax. "Our poor cousin!" exclaimed his hosts. "We do pity you. How can you cut down a tree with a pickax? Obviously, you do not know the difference between a pickax and an ax." "I admit my mistake," the Townsman replied, "but you need not pity me;

instead pity the Blacksmith. I bought only one pickax by mistake, whereas the poor fellow made a whole dozen of them by mistake."

42. The Son-in-Law Who Talked Like an Advocate

Prologue: The Thingazar Sayadaw was visiting Prome and had concluded his sermon for the evening. A young clerk in the office of the British Commissioner, who had studied elementary Pāli in a government school, wanted to air his knowledge before the huge audience and so he addressed the Sayadaw in Pāli, but, as his knowledge of the classical language was very poor, he broke down completely in the middle of a sentence. As the crowd burst into laughter, the Sayadaw said, "Young Layman, continue your study of the Pāli language by all means, but do not practice speaking it on all occasions. You should remember the case of the Son-in-Law who talked like an Advocate."

The only daughter of a Merchant fell in love with a young man, and with the consent of her parents married him. He was without regular employment, being still an apprentice to an Advocate. As they could not afford to have a house of their own, the newly married couple stayed in the Merchant's house. The Son-in-Law proved to be a fine young man, except that, conscious of his chosen profession, he insisted on using in ordinary conversation the stylized language of the courts. This irritated the plain and simple Merchant, his father-in-law.

One night a thief broke into the house, and the Merchant and the Son-in-Law were awakened by the noise. The thief ran away and the two gave chase. As the Son-in-Law was younger and swifter, he was well in front but unfortunately slipped and fell down. The Merchant came running up and asked in urgent tones, "Where has the thief gone?" "My honored father," replied the Son-in-Law slowly and deliberately, "if one can believe one's own eyes, the wicked man, the breaker of the King's Peace, the hardened criminal ran behind those honey-sweet toddy-palm trees standing sentinel over our sleeping village." By the time he had finished speaking, it was too late for the Merchant to go after the thief. Unable to control himself any longer, the Merchant seized hold of his Son-in-Law's neck and, bending him down, gave him a series of poundings on the back with his elbow. The Son-in-Law fell down flat on the ground writing with pain, and the Merchant walked away.

After a few yards, however, the Merchant felt pity for his Son-in-Law. "He is not really a bad young man," he mused. "Moreover, I should not have hurt him so much." So going back to his prostrate Son-in-Law he asked gently, "Have I hurt you, my son?" "Oh cruel, cruel father," the Son-in-Law replied, "because of my evil acts in my previous lives, I have to suffer this assault and battery, to wit, a pounding with the elbow repeated many times over. However, as the tortfeaser is my own beloved father-in-law, my benefactor, the father of my beautiful wife, and the giver of my daily rice, I will not lay a plaint." At this answer, the Merchant shaking with anger, gave his Son-in-Law another pounding with his elbow.

43. The Caravan-Leader Who Bought a Coconut

Prologue: After a sermon at the town of Pyinmana in Middle Burma the Thingazar Sayadaw was told, "We find your lordship's sermons very instructive, but some people say that they contain no deep religious philosophy. In other words, they find the sermons too elementary." The Sayadaw smiled and said, "They remind me of the Caravan-Leader who bought a coconut and found that it was not sweet at all."

During the early days of the kingdom of Ava a caravan of hillmen arrived with their merchandise at the market place. After selling their wares, they went from stall to stall with gold coins jingling in their pockets, looking for rare articles to be bought and taken home.

They paused before a stall selling fruit and looked in wonder at a bunch of coconuts on display. "What are those?" asked the Leader of the Caravan. "Coconuts, my friend," replied the woman stall-keeper. "They are very expensive and only kings and great lords can afford to buy them." "Of course, I can afford to buy them," the Caravan-Leader replied somewhat testily. "Name your price." Learning that the price was one silver coin for one coconut, he bought the whole bunch with a lordly air.

The hillmen then started on their journey homeward and, after one or two days' travel, the Caravan-Leader said, "My friends, let us now taste the wondrous coconut which only kings and lords can eat." So saying, he cut the coconut, ate the outer fiber, and then threw away the nut, thinking it was a mere seed and not dreaming at all that there was sweet milk and a rich kernel inside. His friends followed suit with the other coconuts from the bunch. The Caravan-Leader then said, "Friends, kings and lords are foolish indeed to value this tasteless fruit."

44. Can You Spell "Buffalo"?

Prologue: When the Thingazar Sayadaw was visiting Pyinmana, a town near the Anglo-Burmese border, some laymen informed him that a local scholar wanted to test him on his knowledge of the scriptures. The Thingazar Sayadaw asked them to bring the scholar to him. The laymen went away and came back in the afternoon, but without the scholar. "Where is your learned scholar?" asked the Sayadaw. "He would not come," explained the laymen. "But he has instructed us to ask this question on his behalf: how many *Jatakas* are there in the 550 *Jatakas*?" The Sayadaw smiled and commented, "Your scholar reminds me of the old Abbot in a village on the remote eastern hills."

After the kingdom of Ava had been established the great Monks of the golden city went to remote places in the kingdom to purify and reestablish the religion, which had fallen into neglect and decay during the long period of strife and struggle that followed the breakup of the glorious empire of Pagan.

Those great Monk-missionaries traveled far and wide over the eastern hills, and one of them arrived at a village right on the border of China. He was received by the villagers with respect and hospitality, but with an obvious coldness. They insisted that the religion had never decayed in their village, as their monastery had been continuously occupied by a line of learned abbots. "My lord," they said, "we know that you are learned, but we cannot believe that you are more learned than our own Abbot. Will you agree to hold a disputation with him?" The great Monk from Ava readily agreed.

The villagers with joy and enthusiasm quickly built an alms hall of bamboo and thatch, and placed the great Monk from Ava on a dais. Then they went in procession to the village monastery and brought their Abbot to the alms hall in a sedan chair of velvet and gold. They placed him on another dais. Then the villagers beat their drums and sounded their gongs. At last there was silence, and the master of ceremonies announced, "Now our great Abbot will dispute with the great Monk from Ava."

The great Monk from Ava braced himself to receive a searching and difficult question from the Abbot. There was a pause, and then in a bold firm voice the Abbot asked, "How do you spell 'buffalo'?" The great Monk from Ava was so astonished at this ridiculously simple kindergarten question that he remained speechless. There was again a pause, and then the drums and gongs were beaten again. Cheers and acclamations filled the air, and the master of ceremonies announced that the disputation was now at an end, as the great Monk from Ava had failed to answer the Abbot's question. As the happy villagers carried the Abbot back to the monastery in the sedan chair of gold and velvet, the great Monk and his small band of followers left the village on foot laughing silently to themselves.

45. The Man from Middle Burma

Prologue: Once, when the Thingazar Sayadaw was on a visit to Rangoon, a man came and said, "It seems such a pity, my lord, that there is no conformity of ideas between the various great religions of the world. For example, according to the Buddhist scriptures, in the wink of an eye a billion changes take place in the body of a human being. But according to the Christian belief, the human body was created by God, and so why should such changes take place?" "Layman," replied the monk with a frown, "from your remarks I know that you are neither a devout Christian nor a devout Buddhist. Therefore, there is no point in discussing the matter, and I can only repeat the words of the Headman's Daughter spoken to the Man from Middle Burma: 'You are neither fish nor fowl, you are neither this nor that.' So please do not come again."

The Headman's Daughter was very beautiful and had just attained the age of sixteen. Her ear-boring ceremony had been held, and now young men from the neighborhood would soon come and propose marriage to her. The Headman, therefore, gave her this advice: "Daughter, you are now a mature young woman, and, when young men call to see you, your mother and I will have to retire to the back room, leaving you alone with each young man. It is your privilege to decide whether you will accept a particular young man's proposal of marriage or reject it. They will all be eligible young bachelors and you will have to make your own choice. But beware of young men who come from Middle Burma. The Upper Burman has his virtues and his faults, the Lower Burman also has his virtues and his faults. But men from Middle Burma have no virtues but only faults."

Days passed, and many young men came and proposed marriage to the Headman's Daughter. With each she had a long conversation and then begged for time to decide. Then, one morning, a handsome young man called. The young lady greeted him courteously, and they sat down and conversed for some time. Then the young man, noticing the tiger's skin spread on the floor as a carpet, remarked, "My fair lady, this skin of a water-cat is very beautiful indeed." The young lady looked at him in surprise and thought to herself thus:

"If this man is from Upper Burma, he will know that this is a skin of a tiger, and, if he comes from Lower Burma, he may think it is the skin of a crocodile. But as he refers to a water-cat, it is obvious that he does not know either the tiger or the crocodile, and surely he is from Middle Burma." Remembering her father's advice, she realized that the young man was absolutely unfit to be her future husband, and so she said, "You are neither fish nor fowl, you are neither this nor that. I cannot marry you and so please do not come again."

46. The Ever-Moving Letter "O"

Prologue: When the Thingazar Sayadaw was on a short visit to Myanaung, a town near Henzada, a man dressed in white came and said, "My lord, I was a Buddhist, then I became a Christian, and finally I joined the League of Purity; as a result I am now a devout Buddhist." The Sayadaw smiled and commented, "Layman, you remind me of a poor farmhand who complained that the letter 'O' was always moving."

In a village there once lived a Laborer who could not learn any trade. Since the age of sixteen, he had been an apprentice in various crafts, but, as he was such a dullard, he never could become a journeyman. Now that he was forty years of age, no one would accept him as an apprentice any more, and so he became a common laborer in the household of a farmer.

The Laborer was found absolutely useless in plowing or reaping, or even in herding the cattle. At last he was asked by his disgusted master only to go and catch straying cattle at the close of day. Even in this simple work he failed, because, when herdsmen told him that some cattle had strayed in a particular direction, he could not follow as he did not know which was east and which was west. When he was scolded by his master he replied, "If I only knew which is east, I would be able to find out which is west or north or south." When he was shown by his master a board with the word "east" painted on it, he confessed that he had forgotten completely the letters of the alphabet that he had learned at the monastery so many years before. However, after some thought, he said that he could remember one letter, namely, the letter "O".

So four huge boards were set up near the cattle shed, and one of them had the letter "O" painted on it to indicate the easterly direction. For some days everything went well, for whenever herdsmen told him that some cattle had strayed to the east or west or north or south as the case might be, the Laborer obtained his bearings from the board with the letter "O". Then, some mischievous boys came and painted the letter "O", on the remaining three boards, and the poor Laborer found himself in trouble again. When he was reprimanded by his angry master, the Laborer complained, "But what could I do, master? This "O" seems to move from board to board."

47. The Writing on the Wall

Prologue: A retired government official of Rangoon explained to the Thingazar Sayadaw: "My lord, I am simply bewildered in the maze of religious writings. The more I study religion, the more puzzled I become." "The truth is in the scriptures," replied the Sayadaw. "But, unfortunately, commentators give their own interpretations of the truth. Even the Writing on the Wall by the Village Opium-Eater was interpreted in various ways."

A petty merchant in the village retired from his business, and out of his savings he built a public resthouse near the monastery. He was very proud of his gift, and every morning he came to the resthouse early and swept and cleaned it. He had appealed to the Abbot to warn the monastery boys not to disfigure the resthouse by scrawling and scribbling on the walls with chalk or charcoal. So he became wild with rage when he found one morning the following words written on the wall with charcoal: *Kyût, Môn, Win.* The Resthouse Donor hurried to the monastery and made a violent complaint to the Abbot, who at once followed him to the resthouse to examine the writing on the wall. "Layman" commented the Abbot, "my boys are well disciplined, and, moreover, the writing is so fine and clear that it could never have been written by boys who are just starting to learn the alphabet. In my opinion, the three words constitute a very cryptic message from a person who has renounced the world for the forest this very morning. As you know, the word *Kyût* means 'to be free,' *Môn* means 'to hate,' and *Win* means 'to enter.' Therefore, the message means, 'I have become free, I have learned to hate the pleasures of this world, and I have entered the forest to be away from the abode of men.' " The Resthouse Donor was very pleased with the Abbot's explanation and went around the village boasting that a holy man had stayed in the resthouse for a while before forsaking the world forever.

Soon the resthouse was full of curious villagers, gazing and gaping at the writing on the wall. The Village Physician, the Village Astrologer, and the Village Alchemist were also there. But, in their wisdom, they shook their heads and respectfully disagreed with the Abbot's interpretation. The

Physician said, "This is merely a medical formula. *Kyût* refers to a special kind of mushroom, *Môn* refers to the *gamôn kado* or a sweet-smelling ground orchid, and *Win* refers to *thin win pauk hpu*, a special kind of willow. From these three plants we physicians prepare a medicine which cures all cases of rheumatism." "No, no," interrupted the Astrologer, "the message contains an astrological prediction. As you all know, the letters of our alphabet are divided among the planets. *Kyût* begins with the letter *Ka*, which belongs to the Moon, *Môn* begins with the letter *Ma*, which belongs to Jupiter, and *Win* begins with the letter *Wa*, which belongs to Mercury. In a few weeks' time these three planets will be in the same house, and this message predicts that it will be a time of great good fortune." "Your interpretation is absolutely wrong," asserted the Alchemist. "It is a secret alchemical formula. We base our secret code of alchemic compounds on astrological beliefs. The three letters used in this writing on the wall represent, as you have correctly said, the Moon, Jupiter, and Mercury. But as the Moon rides on a Tiger, Jupiter on a Rat, and Mercury on an Elephant, the writing means 'Free the Tiger, Discard the Rat, and Apply the Elephant.' We alchemists in our secret writings use certain animals to represent the various metals and metal compounds. I cannot divulge the secrets of our group, but I can say that the writing on the wall contains an instruction as to how three particular metal compounds should be processed in our experiments."

The villagers started to argue over the correctness of the four interpretations, but the mystery was soon to be solved. The Village Opium-Eater now arrived at the resthouse, carrying a pail of water and a piece of cloth. He was half asleep and yawning. On being asked the purpose of the pail of water and the piece of cloth, he explained that he had been awakened by his shrewish wife and told to go and see the writing on the wall. "Which writing?" he had asked. "The mysterious words *Kyût, Môn, Win*," replied the wife. When he told her that he himself bad written them the previous night when he was having a quiet smoke on his opium pipe at the resthouse, she had told him to hurry to the resthouse and wash off the writing. The villagers were astounded at this disclosure and for some moments there was silence. Then the Headman of the village asked, "But what do the words mean?" "Sir," replied the Opium-Eater gently, "yesterday I wanted to eat some rice vermicelli, but my wife was cross with me and gave me vegetable broth instead. So, while smoking the opium pipe, I suddenly remembered that, lent having ended, the festival of *Tazaungmôn* would soon be celebrated, and on that occasion, at the nearby *Wingaba* Lake, alms food consisting of rice vermicelli would he served, not only to the venerable monks, but also to the laymen and laywomen present.

So in great joy I scrawled with a piece of charcoal these words *Kyût, Môn, Win*. *Kyût* means 'end' and it refers, of course, to the end of lent; *Môn* stands for the month of *Tazaungmôn*, and Win stands for *Wingaba* Lake."

48. Yesterday, the Hair-Knot; Today, Shaven-Head

Prologue: The Thingazar Sayadaw was on his first visit to Henzada, an important town on the Irrawaddy River, between Prome and Rangoon. He had come with some reluctance, because the people in that locality were great admirers of the Okpo Sayadaw. The two monks were considered to be rivals by their respective followers. It was true that each had bitterly criticized the other, but both monks again and again warned their followers against forming themselves into factions. The Thingazar Sayadaw made it clear to the people of Henzada that he had come with no feeling of animosity against the other monk, and carefully avoided mentioning him in his sermons and in his conversations with the laity, with the result that many who had intended to stay away flocked to hear him preach. One of the most devoted followers of the Okpo Sayadaw was the wife of the township officer appointed by the British. She had asked her companions and friends to stay away from the visiting monk, but now found herself alone in her attempt to boycott the visit. Finally, she herself went to an evening sermon, and at its conclusion said, "My lord, I worship you as I worship the Okpo Sayadaw. I revere you as I revere the Okpo Sayadaw, and I consider you, my lord, as great a monk as the Okpo Sayadaw." "Esteemed Laywoman," the Sayadaw replied, "I feel like the Monk who remonstrated with the Potter's Wife for mentioning his jack fruit tree in her lamentations."

The Potter's Wife had a paramour from another village, and he was a handsome man who wore his long black hair in a topknot. The Potter was in the habit of going to the nearby town on market days to sell his wares, coming home only at midnight. On such days, at nightfall, the paramour would come and lights would be extinguished in the house so that the neighbors could not see inside. The woman was a good cook and took delight in feeding her man with delicious food. One night however, she found that she had forgotten to buy meat, but, so as not to disappoint her lover she killed and cooked the scrawny cockerel, her husband's little pet. The paramour found the chicken curry delicious, but in the darkness he could not see what he was eating, with the result that a large bone became stuck in his throat and choked him to death. The woman was stricken with grief, but she dared not weep aloud in case the neighbors should hear. Then she heard the jingle of bells from her husband's bullock cart and hastily she propped up the dead body in a sitting posture against the kitchen door.

"I am glad you have come back," she greeted her husband, "Chicken thieves must be prowling in the neighborhood, for I hear the dogs barking. So put this spear by the side of your bed, and do sleep lightly." The Potter obediently placed a spear by the side of his bed and fell fast asleep immediately, as he was so tired. After about an hour, and when the moon had risen, she woke him up and whispered, "My dear, there is a man squatting against the kitchen door. The husband jumped out of bed quickly and, seizing the spear, threw it with all his might at the seeming intruder. The dead body fell down on the floor with a big thud and the Wife whispered, "Alas, you have killed him outright. The king's officers will haul you up before the governor and charge you with murder. Now, what shall we do, what shall we do?" The poor Potter was still dazed with sleep and did not know what to do. After a few moments the Wife said brightly, "Husband, be brave. Just carry the dead body into the grounds of the monastery nearby and leave it propped against the jack fruit tree." Accordingly, the Potter dragged the dead body into the monastery grounds and left it propped against the jack fruit tree.

The Monk of the monastery was very fond of jack fruit, and he had often been annoyed by thieves who regularly raided his jack fruit tree. On hearing the footsteps of the Potter, the Monk woke up the Lay Brother and together they saw what seemed to be a man standing against the tree. Seizing two stout cudgels, they ran and beat the dead body until it fell down. "Alas, my lord," exclaimed the Lay Brother, "we have killed him, and the king's officers will arrest us in the morning." "Do not worry," replied the Monk calmly.

"We monks know how to dodge the law." On the Monk's instructions, the Lay Brother shaved off the long hair from the dead man's head and dressed the dead body in the yellow robes of a monk. When morning came the Lay Brother went around the village and announced that a wandering monk had come to the monastery late the previous night, weary and sick, and had suddenly passed away. On hearing the news, the villagers assembled at the monastery to pay their last respects to the dead monk, and among them was the Potter's Wife. On seeing the dead body of her paramour, she could not contain her grief and cried aloud as follows;

"Oh, my handsome beloved,
Yesterday you wore a lovely hair-knot.
Just because you were propped against the jack fruit tree,
Must you become a Shaven-Head?"

On hearing her words, the Monk of the monastery guessed the truth of the whole matter and angrily said to the woman, "Cry on, cry on, and bemoan your paramour, but please do not refer to my jack fruit tree."

49. The Monk and the Farmer's Wife

Prologue: The Thingazar Sayadaw's presence failed to allay the spirit of factionalism and controversy which pervaded Buddhist religious life in Henzada, and so he left the town rather suddenly. An interval of time passed, during which he went on a pilgrimage to Buddha Gaya in India. While he was passing through Rangoon on his return, some laymen from Henzada came and invited the Sayadaw to visit their town again, as the people there were full of remorse for their unjust criticism and the disrespect shown to him on his previous visit. The great monk accepted their invitation, but, on the very evening of his arrival at Henzada, and while he was giving his first sermon to a very large audience, an open attempt was made on his life. A man suddenly stood up from among the audience and emptied his double-barreled gun at the Sayadaw. There was a commotion, but the Sayadaw calmly went on preaching, and the would-be assassin escaped. The mystery of this incident remains unsolved to the present day. According to one version, the man was chased and caught, but the monk interceded with the captors to let the culprit go. It was obvious that the man was merely a tool, and in those days a double-barreled gun was a rarity and was owned only by officials serving the new British government. Many suspected of complicity those laymen who went to Rangoon and invited the monk to Henzada. The Okpo Sayadaw himself came and paid his respects to the Thingazar Sayadaw, expressing his dismay and regret at the unseemly incident. The Thingazar Sayadaw gave no more sermons and left Henzada when the excitement over the attempted assassination had died down. Some weeks later the same group of laymen followed the Sayadaw to Rangoon and invited the monk to make yet another visit to Henzada. The Sayadaw smiled and said, "I want to come, but like the Shaven-Head who once loved a Farmer's Wife, I am so afraid, I am so afraid."

On the outskirts of a village there lived a Farmer and his Wife. His paddy field was some distance away and so every day he had to leave his house before dawn together with his two plow oxen, thus leaving his Wife all alone except for their small child. There was a monastery nearby which was occupied by a single Monk, and he also was in the habit of rising before dawn to chant his scriptures. So every morning at early dawn, before the neighbors had woken up, the Woman would sing her lullaby, beginning with the words "Hush-a-bye, my baby," and in the nearby monastery the Monk would chant his recitations, beginning with the words "Happiness be to all beings." After some time the two began to feel that they were companions and friends; later they became lovers. The Woman's lullaby then became a signal that the coast was clear, and the Monk's chant the signal that he would be with her in a few moments.

However, the course of true love never did run smooth, and neighbors will be neighbors. They soon suspected that there was a romance between the Farmer's Wife and the Monk, and warned the Farmer that lonely wives were not always virtuous. So one morning the Farmer purposely left behind his bamboo helmet and went off to the fields. Then the Wife and the Monk exchanged their signal tunes, and soon he was with her. At that moment, however, they heard the Farmer's footsteps and his voice shouting out, "Wife, I have come back for my helmet!" Hastily, the Wife looked for a place to hide her lover and, seeing a huge rice jar, pushed the Monk into it. But, alas, the jar was too small for him to squat down and too low for him to stand up. He wriggled himself in, but the top of his shaven dome remained visible. Refusing to admit defeat, the woman swiftly seized a winnowing sieve and jammed it down on the Monk's head. The woman was strong and the Monk's skull thick, so the shaven dome cut a hole in the center of the sieve and protruded out of it.

The Farmer now entered the kitchen, and, on looking round, saw the protruding shaven dome. "What is that strange object on the top of the rice jar?" he asked innocently. "It is an old gong I bought at the market the other day," replied the Wife sweetly, "and I am using it as a lid for the rice jar." Saying that he wanted to test the tone of the gong, the Fanner beat the protruding head with his driving stick, but no sound came because the Monk bit his lips and stopped himself from giving a howl of pain. "Strange indeed," exclaimed the Farmer, "I have never come across a silent gong and I must test it again." The Farmer's Wife thought that the Monk was acting stupidly and she whispered, "Gong, are you dumb?" So, when the Farmer hit the shaven head again with the driving stick, an impressive sound of "Doo-oo-oo" came from inside the jar. The Farmer went on giving stroke after stroke with his stick, and every time the poor Monk had to give out a sound in imitation of a gong. Satisfied that he had taught the Monk a lesson, the Farmer went back to his field, and the Monk returned to his monastery.

The next morning everything was back to normal. The Farmer left the house at the usual hour and the Wife made sure that he had not forgotten anything this time. So after an interval, she sang out:

"Hush-a-bye, my baby,
 Do go to sleep,
 Your father is gone
 To sow and to reap."

But the Monk chanted back as follows:

"Happiness be to all,
 I dare not come to you;
 Remembering yesterday,
 I dread the doo-oo-oo!"

50. Master Talkative and His Dark-Skinned Wife

Prologue: When the Thingazar Sayadaw was on a visit to Bassein an enthusiastic scholar of Buddhist scriptures expressed his strong desire to introduce certain drastic reforms in the practice of religion in the country. "My lord," he argued, "take the case of the Precepts. People keep the Five Precepts on ordinary days and the Eight Precepts or the Ten Precepts on Sabbath days. They have forgotten the great value of the Nine Precepts. In my opinion, my lord, the Five and the Eight Precepts do not go far enough, and the Ten Precepts are difficult to keep because they include the Precept of refraining from taking nourishment after the hour of noon. I cannot understand why the lord monks have not reminded their followers to take the Nine Precepts. For myself, I keep the Nine Precepts every day, and will you not, my lord, preach a sermon on the subject?" "Why is the Precept against taking nourishment after noontide difficult to keep?" asked the Sayadaw. "Because men have to work at all hours of the day and without proper meals they cannot work," the scholar answered. "Then why do you not forsake the world and become a monk like me?" the monk questioned. "I cannot forsake my family," explained the scholar. "You despise the world and yet you cannot leave it," the Sayadaw commented. "Moreover, my lord," the scholar continued to argue, "why do people follow their customs so blindly? Just because my father and my mother and my grandparents kept the Five Precepts on ordinary days and the Eight or Ten Precepts on the Sabbath days, is that any reason why I should not keep the Nine Precepts every day?" "Layman," the monk said, "old practices are not easy to discard, as Master Talkative found to his cost when he attempted to divorce his Wife."

aster Talkative had been married to his wife, a dark-skinned lady called Mistress Golden, for some ten years, but one day he saw a young girl with a fair complexion and fell in love with her. So he wanted to divorce his wife, but she refused to agree. He then decided to play a trick on her and said, "Dear Golden, I consulted an astrologer today and he told me that we are star-crossed and, unless we part, one of us will die. Therefore, it is necessary for us to have a 'to-please-the-stars' divorce." Mistress Golden asked for time to consider the matter, and went and consulted the neighbors, who explained to her that, according to law, a "to-please-the-stars" divorce was not a real divorce but merely a temporary separation, but that, if either the husband or the wife refused to return at the end of three months, it automatically became a valid divorce. Realizing that her husband intended not to return, she refused to consent to the suggested "to-please-the-stars" divorce.

Nothing daunted, Master Talkative engaged a famous lawyer from Pegu and sued his wife for divorce. Mistress Golden on her part engaged a famous lawyer from Pagan to defend her case. When the suit came up before the judge, the lawyer from Pegu pointed out that Mistress Golden, in spite of her name, was a dark-skinned woman, and asked:

"Mistress Golden
  Black as lead.
  May my client
  Leave her bed?"

The Lawyer from Pagan stood up, smoothed his robes, and replied;

"She was jet black
  Ten years ago.
  Could she change
  To color of snow?"

The judge decided that a dark complexion was never a ground for divorce and, in addition, that the lady was dark at the time of the marriage ten years ago and had remained consistently dark. Accordingly, he dismissed the suit and passed orders making Master Talkative liable for costs.

51. A Forest-Dweller Should Know How To Sing and Dance

Prologue: Many monks were leaving the monasteries of Mandalay for the rocky cliffs of Sagaing on the other bank of the Irrawaddy River. Although the pioneers of the movement migrated there to escape from the bustle of city life, and to live in caves and recesses, their imitators went only because they wanted to dwell in the new monasteries built on the cliffs by enthusiastic donors. The town of Sagaing grew in size and population, so that it came to possess an atmosphere similar to that of the golden city on the other side of the river. One day the Thingazar Sayadaw overheard his followers extolling those monks who had migrated to Sagaing as forest dwellers shunning cities, towns, and villages. The Sayadaw pointed out that, as the so-called caves of Sagaing were merely monasteries built on the cliffsides, the monks dwelling there could not be described as "forest dwellers." "Moreover," he continued, "mere dwelling in the forest or in caves is not a sign of piety, for surely rabbits living in their burrows in the forest could not be considered to be pious and austere." Finally, he told them the tale of the Forest-Dwelling Monk.

Some villagers going to the forest near their village to gather firewood were surprised to find a newly built hut of bamboo and thatch, but their surprise turned to joy when they saw an old monk sitting inside it telling his beads. "He is a Forest-Dwelling Monk," they exclaimed, "and he must have come to this forest and built this little hut-monastery with his own hands so as to be away from villages and towns." They went back to their village and brought their relations and friends to worship the pious recluse and to offer him alms. "We must not disturb him in his meditation," the villagers agreed among themselves. "We will bring alms every morning but will not stay long. Even on Sabbath days we will not stay beyond the hour of noon."

The simple villagers had no inkling of the real reason why the monk had come to dwell in the forest. He had entered the order only after he had retired from his business as a merchant. He was both too old and too lazy to begin studying the scriptures, and he found his position in the monastery difficult; first, he felt awkward living with monks who were much younger than himself in years but much senior to him in rank and learning, and, second, lay visitors to the monastery, thinking that he was a senior monk, judging from his age and appearance, often asked him to give them a sermon, and he felt ashamed when he had to refuse their request. After some thought, he decided that the best thing for him was to live alone in a makeshift hut in the forest, far away from learned monks and sermon-wanting laymen.

For his first few months as a Forest-Dweller, everything went well with the monk. He received regular offerings of alms food in the morning and was respected, admired, and loved by the villagers. On Sabbath days he was asked only to give the formula of the Ten Precepts, and, as the villagers left by noon, there was never time or occasion for a sermon. However, as months went by, he found his life as a Forest-Dweller rather irksome. He had no scriptures to read, no abstruse point to ponder upon, and no meditative exercise to perform. He tried to tell his beads, but found that he could not concentrate. As a young man he used to be a good singer and a good dancer, and even as a busy merchant he had found time to dance and sing regularly before friends. Now alone, and with no particular task to perform, surely he would not do any harm to anybody if he should sing and dance to while away his leisure hours. So every day, through the long afternoons, he sang and danced by himself in the privacy of his little hut-monastery.

All would have gone well with the Forest-Dweller to the end of his life, except for a wayward bull. It was a Sabbath day and all the villagers had come to take the Ten Precepts and had gone. In the village the children were sleeping and the elders were resting, and the farm animals were tied up. Alone in his little hut-monastery, the Forest-Dweller was singing and dancing. But before the afternoon had advanced, a wayward bull gnawed through the ropes, jumped over the fence, and wandered away towards the forest. Its owner chased it and caught it near the hut-monastery. After tying the bull to a tree, the villager walked towards the hut to get a drink of water, as he felt so thirsty from running in the sun. "I must go softly," he said to himself, "so as not to disturb the venerable monk in his meditation or prayer." As the villager drew nearer to the hut he was surprised to hear the following song:

"Step with the left foot, step with the right,
 The sparkle from my yellow robes sets fire to the clouds.
 King of gods, are you anxious?
 Then step with the left foot, step with the right,
 And kick the sparkle back to me."

The puzzled villager rushed into the hut and found the Forest-Dweller standing on one leg, with the other curled up. The Forest-Dweller hastily sat down and, hoping that the simple villager had guessed nothing, said, "Layman, on this Sabbath day, have you come here to become a Forest-Dweller like myself?" The villager replied in disapproval, "My lord; I am not qualified to be a Forest-Dweller, because I can neither dance nor sing."

52. The Origin of Conical Hats

Prologue: The Thingazar Sayadaw and a group of laymen were discussing the new sects which had suddenly appeared in Lower Burma. One of the laymen asked, "My lord, before the advent of King Anawrahta, the monks used to wear conical hats. How did conical hats originate?" The Sayadaw replied, "Layman, the scriptures made no mention of conical hats, and our ancient chronicles did not record how those hats first came into being. I can, however, tell you a tale which you must not believe to be absolutely true. A teller of tales has to use a little imagination. I will illustrate my point with an example: a person was giving an account of a fight at dead of night, and near his house, between two wolves; he concluded with a statement that one of the animals ran away with a broken leg; on being asked how he knew that the leg was broken, he gave the explanation that a nightbird had told him. I will now give you an account of the origin of the conical hats, but, should you ask me how I knew, I would have to reply that a little nightbird told me."

In the early days of Pagan, long before the great Anawrahta came to its throne, there lived an Abbot, who was also the King's teacher. One morning he woke up with a start and found a pair of horns growing on his head. Feeling ashamed, he slipped into the kitchen, and out of some trays and baskets he made a conical hat and wore it on his head so as to hide the horns. To his relief, nobody made any comment on his conical hat or asked him why he was wearing it. But he kept worrying in case his secret should be discovered. After some days, he felt he could not stand the anxiety any longer, and, after informing the King that he wanted to be a forest dweller, he retired to the thickest part of the nearby forest. There, in a little monastery of bamboo and thatch he spent his days alone, receiving his alms food from the Lay Brother who came to him every morning.

One morning the Lay Brother arrived unusually early and found the Abbot without the conical hat on his head. Noticing the protruding horns, the Lay Brother cried out in alarm, "Calm yourself, Lay Brother," said the Abbot. "It is my misfortune to have these horns on my head, but, as long as only you and I know, no harm is done. I put you on oath not to tell it to anybody." The Lay Brother kept quiet, but on his return journey through the forest he could not contain himself any longer, and, thinking that no one was about, he shouted to the winds, "An awful thing has happened! Two horns have appeared on my Abbot's head! Two horns have appeared on the head of the great King's Teacher!" Unknown to the distraught Lay Brother, at that very moment a hunter was taking aim with his crossbow at a deer. The deer, frightened by the Lay Brother's loud shout, darted away.

The disappointed hunter returned to the city and informed the butchers of his inability to supply them with venison for the day. The butchers became angry and threatened to sue him for breach of contract. "But, friends," the hunter explained, "it was not my fault at all. A strange voice in the forest, telling that the King's Teacher, the Abbot, had horns on his head, frightened away the deer that I would certainly have killed." As the result of the hunter's disclosure, the story of the Abbot's horns spread through the city until it reached the ears of the King himself.

The King was distressed and sent gongsmen round the city to announce that the story about the Abbot's horns was not true. This resulted in bitter controversy, some people saying that such a learned and pious monk could not have horns on his head, while others said that there never was any smoke without a fire and that the King should himself go and examine the head of his Teacher. At last the King called for his elephant and, riding it, he went to the forest-monastery. On seeing the King approaching, the Abbot threw away his conical hat and sat down on the floor with downcast eyes. The King came into the monastery and was shocked to see the two horns on his Teacher's head. Grief-stricken, ashamed, annoyed, and angry, he forgot dignity, decorum, and respect, and, crying "How can this happen to my venerable Teacher?", tugged at the horns. Surprisingly the horns came apart from the head. Abbot and King, Teacher and Pupil jumped up in joy, and together they returned in triumph to the city.

53. Master Doll Who Journeyed to Rangoon To Sell Tobacco Leaves

Prologue: The Thingazar Sayadaw was visiting a town in the Irrawaddy delta. The townspeople were divided into two rival groups, one supporting the orthodox sect and the other the Okpo sect. Some elders pleaded with the Sayadaw to call up both groups and to exhort them to live in peace and harmony. The Sayadaw, in addressing the members of the two groups, explained to them that the point of controversy between the two sects was of very little importance and that therefore the two sects were almost identical in belief and practice, "as identical as Rangoon and Prome were to Master Doll who went to Rangoon to sell tobacco leaves."

Once there lived in the town of Prome a man by the name of Master Doll, and the name fitted his character, because he was dull, good-natured, and quiet. In contrast, his wife Mistress Stout was intelligent, strong-willed, and efficient. They owned a small tobacco plantation, and, hearing that the price of tobacco leaves was very high in Rangoon, Mistress Stout suggested to her husband that he should make a journey to Rangoon with two baskets full of tobacco. "But I do not know the way," Master Doll protested, "and I cannot go by boat or by cart, as the cost of passage will be greater than the little profit I can make." "Rangoon is only one hundred and twenty miles away," Mistress Stout replied. "Surely you are a man and can walk that little distance." "I am very bad at remembering directions," Master Doll continued to protest, "and I shall surely lose my way." "You need not worry yourself on that account," Mistress Stout replied. "Just weave two baskets, one very big and the other very small and fill them with tobacco leaves."

After two or three days the two baskets had been woven and were duly filled with tobacco leaves. Mistress Stout put a carrying pole on her husband's shoulder and strung the big basket at the front end and the smaller one at the back end. After leading him to the high road and making him face the direction where Rangoon was, she instructed, "Follow the big basket. When you eat or sleep on the way, carefully place the baskets on the ground so that the big one will always be in the direction of Rangoon."

Master Doll slowly walked along the high road until the sun set and darkness fell. Carefully putting down the baskets according to his wife's instructions, he ate his dinner which Mistress Stout had lovingly packed for him before he left his house. Then he went to sleep on the roadside. An hour or two later a bullock-cart came by, and the cartman was very annoyed to find the two baskets blocking the way. He tried to wake the sleeping traveler without success. The cartman said to himself, "Poor old fellow, he must be very tired and I will not trouble him." So saying, he moved the two baskets to the roadside and continued his journey. But alas for Master Doll, the cartman had placed the two baskets in the reverse order with the big basket lying in the direction of Prome.

At early dawn Master Doll woke up refreshed. After carefully shouldering the carrying pole, he faithfully followed his dear wife's instructions and walked with the big basket in front. By nightfall he reached Prome again. The simple Master Doll, thinking he had arrived in Rangoon, silently congratulated himself for having made the long journey in two days. At the same time he felt disappointed because, contrary to the tales he had heard, Rangoon seemed to be as dull as Prome. "Where are the big ships? And where are the brick houses?" he asked himself. "Even their great Shwedagon Pagoda is no bigger than our own Shwesandaw Pagoda." As he walked slowly on, he was surprised to find that the streets and houses were identical with the streets and houses of Prome. He was even more surprised when he found a street exactly like his own street and a house on it exactly like his own house. Stopping in front of it, he called out, "Good Householder, please come out and assist a poor benighted traveler."

Mistress Stout looked out of the window and saw her husband. Saying "Why has the old man returned?", she went down to the gate. Master Doll was now truly amazed and he asked in great excitement, "Happy denizen of Rangoon, you look exactly like my wife. May I inquire whether you have any relation at Prome by the name of Mistress Stout, wedded to the tobacco-seller Master Doll?" Making no reply, Mistress Stout seized hold of the topknot on Master Doll's head and, bending him down, beat his back with the ladle she happened to be holding. Then she said, "You old Doll, you old dumb Doll! Can you not recognize that this is Prome, this is your house, and this is your wife?" Without a word Master Doll went into the house and came back with a long knife. As the wife cowered in fear, he cut the big basket into pieces, and, turning round to his wife with a smile, he said sweetly, "The big basket misled me."

54. The Monk Who Hated Music

Prologue: When the Thingazar Sayadaw was visiting Rangoon a man came up to him and said, "My lord, the younger monks of Rangoon have banded themselves into a new sect known as the Junior Sect. They are determined to introduce reforms in the order. They refuse to attend any religious ceremony if an orchestra or a dancing troupe is present. To listen to music or to watch a dance is strictly against the rules of the order, and surely my lord will exhort the older monks of the city not to attend any religious ceremony where dancers or musicians are present?" The Sayadaw smiled and commented, "I am afraid that the Junior Monks hate music and dancing in the same way as the Monk Puppet Showman hated music and dancing!"

A puppet showman, famous for his music and song, suddenly retired from his profession and became a monk. But people could not forget his fame as a puppet showman, and called him Monk Puppet Showman.

Monk Puppet Showman did not become very learned in the scriptures nor did he practice any special austerity. In other words, he was a very ordinary monk. However, he refused to attend any religious ceremony where there was any dancing or music. "I hate the very sound of music," he declared again and again.

In a few weeks this particular abstinence of Monk Puppet Showman won for him many admirers. "Even great abbots do not abstain from going to religious ceremonies where musicians and dancers perform," people commented. After a few months a rich villager built and donated a special monastery for the Monk. Some years passed and the Monastery-Donor wanted to hold the initiation ceremony of his only son in pomp and splendor. By common custom, Monk Puppet Showman was invited to preside over the ceremony. As usual, the Monk insisted that he hated the very sound of music, and accepted the invitation to be present at the ceremony on the distinct understanding that there was to be no music or song or dance. The appointed day arrived, and everything was now ready for the initiation ceremony. The young men of the village, however, were in a mutinous mood, for, they asked, "Whoever heard of an initiation ceremony without dance or song?" They became so persistent with their protests that the Monastery-Donor finally agreed to engage a drummer who would play a mere "slow march" on the long drum.

There was no time to inform Monk Puppet Showman of the new arrangement; moreover, the Monastery-Donor thought that there could not be any objection on the part of the Monk against the presence of a single drummer. Monk Puppet Showman soon arrived leading a procession of monks, walking slowly and sedately, and with downcast eyes. The drummer started to play the drum, and Monk Puppet Showman, on hearing the sound of the drum, exclaimed, "The reason why I hate the sound of music is because it incites me to dance. But the harm is now done. So, drummer, stop your royal march and play a jig." The drummer did as told, and Monk Puppet Showman, gathering up his robes, danced his way into the almsgiving hall.

55. I Ran Because the Other Ran

Prologue: While the Thingazar Sayadaw was visiting Pegu, a layman announced that he was an admirer of the Chapter of Junior Monks. "Why do you admire them?' asked the Sayadaw. "My lord," replied the layman, "I have no particular reasons. My neighbor admires them, and I simply follow suit." "You are like the Hillman," smiled the Sayadaw, "who ran because the Other ran."

On a road among the eastern hills a Burmese Traveler heard a Hillman shouting out his ware, which happened to be rice. But, as he was shouting in his own language, the Burmese Traveler did not understand and asked, "What is it? What is it?" The Hillman of course knew Burmese, but like most Hillmen, he spoke it with a twang. To enlighten the Burmese stranger, he shouted the Burmese word for rice.

The Burmese word for rice was *sunn*, but, because of his twang, it sounded like *sinn*, which meant "elephant." So the Burmese Traveler thought that the Hillman was warning him of an approaching wild elephant, and started to run as fast as he could. The Hillman, although perplexed at the Burman's behavior, ran behind him. The sun was hot and the road was rough. About an hour later the two arrived at a village, and both fell down in a swoon through sheer exhaustion.

After the two strangers had been nursed back to consciousness, the villagers asked, "Why did you come running so hard? Did robbers waylay you, or did some wild animal chase you?" "This Hillman here warned me of an approaching wild elephant," explained the Burman. The Hillman looked at his fellow runner with amazement and denied that he had ever given such a warning. "Then why did you run?" the villagers asked. "It was quite simple," replied the Hillman. "I ran because he ran."

56. The Mad Abbot and His Confessional

Prologue: The Thingazar Sayadaw was visiting Pegu, an important town in Lower Burma, and one of his former pupils, now a fully ordained monk, came to see him. The young monk said, "I know that my lord will disapprove of my action, but I must inform your lordship that I have become a member of the Junior Chapter." "What were your reasons for joining it?" the Sayadaw asked. "I found that people in this town give more alms to the monks of the Junior Chapter," the young monk replied. The Sayadaw smiled and commented, "A similar reason prompted a young monk to join the Confessional of a mad Abbot."

The Abbot of a village monastery became queer in his head, and one by one the other monks left the monastery. At last even the lay brother went away, and the Abbot thus became the only occupant of the monastery. However, as the Abbot in spite of his madness retained his dignity and decorum, the villagers, remembering his past learning and piety, still brought him their offerings of alms food every morning.

One day two monks arrived at the village. They were on a pilgrimage to the various pagodas of the region, and, through some miscalculation of the time and the distance, reached the village only half an hour before noon. As there was not enough time for them to go round the village with their begging bowls, they knocked at the door of the monastery. The mad Abbot opened the door and gave them welcome. "We are pilgrims, my lord," explained the strangers. "The hour of noon is fast approaching, and yet we have not broken our fast." "I have enough alms food for both of you," replied the Abbot. "Before we take our meal, however, assist me to hold a Confessional. I reside here alone and no monks have visited me for some weeks, with the result that I have not been able to confess my misdemeanors."

The Abbot and the two strangers sat down together. Suddenly the Abbot jumped up. Then, raising his right hand and his left leg in the posture of a dance, he sang:

> "March is past,
> April is here,
> The sun is hot,
> The sky is clear."

He stopped in the middle of the song, and, looking angrily at the seated monks, shouted, "You are imposters! You must be imposters and not monks at all, because you do not know how to take part in a Confessional. Unless you join me in the holding of the Confessional, I will request the village headman to send a horseman to the ecclesiastical censor in the golden city, soliciting permission to put you under arrest immediately."

The mad Abbot, raising his right hand and his left leg, sang again:

> "March is past,
> April is here,
> The sun is hot,
> The sky is clear."

The younger of the two monks now jumped up, and, raising his left arm and right leg, he concluded the Abbot's song with the following lines:

> "Cover your shaven head,
> Oh, my Abbot dear."

As the Abbot clapped his hands and cheered, and the Younger Monk continued to sing and dance, the Older Monk left the monastery in disgust. Going to the nearest cottage, he stood still with his begging bowl. The owner of the cottage, seeing the monk, invited him in with the following words, "The sun is almost overhead, and we have eaten our breakfast long ago. Luckily we have a few bananas and some tea, which we will offer immediately." The Older Monk ate the bananas and drank the tea. After giving the Five Precepts to the cottager and his family, he proceeded to the nearby resthouse and waited for his fellow pilgrim. Soon the Younger Monk came out of the monastery and joined him. "You ought to be ashamed of yourself," the Older Monk scolded. "But my lord, my lord," the Younger Monk pleaded, "I was so hungry and the alms food smelled so nice."

57. The Ecclesiastical Censor Who Lost His Self

Prologue: Just after the Thingazar Sayadaw had concluded his sermon, a pompous-looking lay preacher asked, "My lord, please preach to me and teach me to lose the illusion of self." The Sayadaw, realizing at once that the man, wanting to air his knowledge of the scriptures, was merely seeking an opportunity to argue and dispute, forestalled him by this reply: "Learned layman, I feel tired after my sermon and, moreover, I do not wish you to become like the Ecclesiastical Censor who lost his Self."

The Ecclesiastical Censor was as learned in the scriptures as all ecclesiastical censors had to be. Like all ecclesiastical censors, he was also pitiless and merciless, and a faithful servant of his King. One evening, as he roamed the streets in search of his prey, namely wayward monks, he caught a little Novice who, being homesick, had slipped out of the monastery to see his mother. "Halt!" the Censor commanded. "What is my lord doing in the darkness of the night and on a public road?" "Great Official," the Novice replied with a trembling voice. "I am only a Novice, and I have been home to see my mother. I assure you that I am now on my way back to the monastery." "I put you under arrest," the Censor replied gruffly. "Lead me to your Abbot, and I will lay a charge against you."

The poor frightened Novice led the haughty Censor to the monastery. From outside the closed gates, the Censor shouted, "Open, in the name of the King! The great Ecclesiastical Censor wishes to see the Abbot and lay a charge against a wayward monk." The Lay Brother in charge of the gates looked out through the peephole and saw the Censor with his captive, the trembling Novice. So as to give the little Novice a chance to escape, the Lay Brother boldly replied, "Great Censor, our Abbot is at prayers and cannot be disturbed. Without his authority I cannot open the gates. Please come in the morning."

The Ecclesiastical Censor was in a towering rage, but he realized fully that even the King himself had not the power to break open the gates, unless some grave act of immorality or breach of discipline had occurred within the monastery. As it was now nearly midnight, he decided to spend the night in the nearby public resthouse. "Remember that you are under arrest, Novice," he warned, "and if you attempt to run away I will charge you with high treason." Then the Censor sat down, leaning his back against a post and glaring at the unhappy Novice. After an hour or two, in spite of himself, the Censor fell asleep.

The little Novice thought to himself, "If I run away now, when the morning dawns he will demand my surrender from the Abbot. So I must think of a way to trick him." He racked his brains, until in his desperation he hit on a brilliant idea. By this time the Censor was in such a deep sleep that he was snoring with his mouth agape. Swiftly the Novice stripped the Censor naked and wrapped him in his own yellow robes. Then, dressed in the Censor's clothes, the Novice ran to the gates of his monastery and was let in by the watching Lay Brother.

When morning broke, the Censor woke up and was furious to find himself dressed in yellow robes and the Novice gone. He hurried to the gates of the monastery and, announcing his identity, demanded to see the Abbot. "How could you be the Great Censor?" the Lay Brother asked innocently. "You must be the wayward Novice whom the great official arrested last night. Did you lie to him to make him think you belonged to our monastery? Go away, go away before the Great Censor catches you again." "But I am the Great Censor," the Censor insisted. "Then where is the Novice you arrested last night?" questioned the Lay Brother. "He has disappeared," the Censor replied sheepishly. "In that case, Great Censor," jeered the Lay Brother, "you have lost your self and have become the Novice instead." Feeling defeated and ashamed, the Censor returned to the resthouse and hid himself among the rafters. Only at nightfall did he muster enough courage to run back as fast as he could to his own house.

58. Disputations with King Mindon

THE MONK AND THE PLANK

The Thingazar Sayadaw and King Mindon had been closeted together for some hours, disputing over certain points from the scriptures. When the Sayadaw came out from the debating chamber, the Chief Minister respectfully inquired, "How did my lord fare in the disputation with the King?" The Sayadaw replied, "Great Minister, my debate with His Majesty reminds me of the Monk and the plank. Once, in a monastery situated on the bank of a river, there lived a Monk who could not swim. Becoming tired of having to just sit and watch the other monks swim, he jumped into the river, holding a long plank in his hands. Once in the water, he tried to ride on the plank, but, contrary to his expectations, he found that he could not keep his seat for long, and so sometimes the Monk was on the plank and at other times the plank was on the Monk. In the same way, during our disputation, sometimes I was on top of the King, but at other times the King was on top of me."

THE GLORY OF EMPEROR ASOKA

The great Abbots of Mandalay, including the Thingazar Sayadaw, were gathered in the palace after an almsgiving by the King, and they recited certain portions of the scriptures. King Mindon was in a bad mood and commented, "My lords, I doubt whether your recitation of the scriptures is really effective. In the days of the Great Emperor Asoka, when the monks recited the scriptures on royal request, the recitation was so potent that the drinking water in jars in front of them bubbled and boiled. But the drinking water in the jars in front of my lords remains placid and cool as ever." This expression of displeasure by the King was received in silence by other monks, but the Thingazar Sayadaw would not let it pass without his comment. "Your Majesty," he said, "the Great Emperor Asoka ruled over not only human beings but also the dragons of the sea. He could command even the king of the dragons to appear before him. But Your Majesty cannot command even a grass snake." King Mindon, clapping his hands, laughed loudly and apologized to the assembled monks for his insulting remarks.

THE BOWMAN

After listening to an amusing story told by the Thingazar Sayadaw, King Mindon said, "My lord's stories are simply wonderful. But they are so wonderful that sometimes I suspect that my lord spends many hours composing them long before they are actually delivered." "Great King," replied the Sayadaw, "when a hunter roams the forest in search of game, he has his crossbow ready, but he sets it and takes aim only when he sees his quarry. In the same way, I make up my story only when I notice an amusing personality or a comic situation."

THE WESTERN WING OF THE PALACE

King Mindon was in a happy mood, and, wanting to tease the great Abbots, said, "As my lords are aware, the western wing of my palace contains the private apartments of the queens and their ladies, and no man except myself can have access to it. But my lords are great Abbots, whose manly fires of passion have been quenched long ago. So when my lords leave this audience chamber after partaking of the alms food, will they please go through the western wing." As the Abbots made no reply, the King taunted them with these words, "My lords, I suspect that your manly fires of passion have not been quenched after all, and my lords dare not pass through my ladies' apartments."

"Great King," replied the Thingazar Sayadaw, "through the window I can see the hills lying to the east. Although only a few miles away from this parched city, the hills are cool with their thickly forested slopes and rippling waterfalls. But strangers seldom go there, because of the danger of contracting malarial fever. Doubtless the western wing of this golden palace is cool and shady, but we would not like to visit it, in case we should contract a royal malady." The King clapped his hands and roared with laughter.

THE ANCIENT PAGODA

King Mindon complained to the Thingazar Sayadaw: "My lord, I find the other Abbots orthodox, old-fashioned, and behind the times. My engineers, building a straight road from the city to the shore, have applied to me for permission to demolish an ancient pagoda which they find to be in their way, offering at the same time to rebuild the pagoda at a more suitable place. The great Abbots, however, say that, as the pagoda is not yet in ruins and is still being used as a place of worship by the people, it will be improper to demolish it. My lord is famous for liberal opinions, and I am sure my lord will say that it is perfectly proper for the engineers to demolish the ancient shrine." "Of course, it is proper," agreed the Sayadaw readily. "But a certain condition will have to be fulfilled. In demolishing the pagoda, your engineers must not break a single brick." King Mindon clapped his hands, laughed, and said, "All right, my lord, the ancient pagoda will not be demolished."

THE KING BEMOANS HIS KINGSHIP

King Mindon was in a discontented mood. "My lord," he said, "life is continuous suffering. I suffer because I am King, I suffer because I live in a golden palace, and I suffer because I am surrounded by handsome lords and gracious ladies." The Thingazar Sayadaw smiled and commented, "Your Majesty's remarks remind me of Schoolboy More-and-More and his Uncle the great Abbot."

Once in a village monastery there lived a schoolboy by the name of More-and-More. Unlike other boys living and studying in the monastery, he was not at all afraid of the Abbot, who was only his father's younger brother. One Sabbath day some laymen came with an offering of rice gruel for all the inmates of the monastery. For others it was ordinary rice gruel, but for the Abbot it was rice gruel mixed with milk and honey. More-and-More's mouth watered as he watched his uncle eat the special gruel. The Abbot, as he swallowed spoonful after spoonful, exclaimed, "All is suffering, all is suffering. This vile body has to be fed. To eat is suffering, to swallow is suffering." More-and-More looked at his uncle in astonishment and commented, "Such sufferings More-and-More will always welcome."

The lords and ladies in waiting laughed aloud at the Sayadaw's tale and the King, blushing deeply, joined in the laughter.

THE VILLAGER AND THE CHICKEN CURRY

King Mindon said to the assembled great Abbots, "My lords, every Sabbath day after the offering of alms food, I listen to your lordships' sermons. The sermons are wonderful, and I never tire of listening to them. But I am very stupid, and I wonder whether I can ever learn even the elementary essentials of Buddhism." While the other Abbots remained silent, the Thingazar Sayadaw replied, "We trust Your Majesty is not merely trying to find an excuse to be absent from the Sabbath day sermons, and I hope Your Majesty will never be like the Villager who ate up all the chicken curry."

The Villager came home from the fields very hungry and was delighted to find that his Wife had prepared for his dinner delicious chicken curry. In no time he finished a plateful of rice and chicken curry, and asked for some more. His Wife replied, "I have another plateful of rice, but you will have to eat it with only garlic and salt, for there is no more chicken curry except a small bowlful which I am going to take to my parents later in the evening." "But, dear Wife," replied the Villager, "your parents are by no means starving, and surely they must have cooked their own curry. "Husband," explained the

Wife. "I know that they do not need anything from us, but I cannot forget even for a moment the great debt of gratitude I owe to them for their love and care." "Dear Wife," said the Villager, "you do owe a mountain of gratitude and your debt to your parents is so great that you can never repay it. So why try with a little bowl of chicken curry?" So saying, he seized hold of the bowl and ate up its contents.

THE DRAIN

King Mindon said to the assembled Abbots, "My lords, my Ecclesiastical Censor has reported to me that there has been a marked increase in the number of monks found to be lax not only in discipline but also in morals. According to him, serious breaches of discipline and morals are occurring not only in remote towns but in this golden city itself. With the full consent and cooperation of my lords, I propose to authorize my Ecclesiastical Censor to take rigid measures against those pseudo monks who are unworthy to wear the yellow robe." Before others could reply, a very senior Abbot remarked, "Your Majesty, there is no doubt that there are many who wear the yellow robe but do not keep the vows of the order. We are living in a decadent period of our history, and, in spite of all the measures that Your Majesty can take, there will always be wicked men wearing the yellow robe and pretending to be monks." The King was obviously disheartened by these words. Then the Thingazar Sayadaw said, "My lord Abbot, in the backyard of our monastery there is a drain in which is thrown all the filth and rubbish of the monastery, and in the morning the lay brothers and novices clean out the drain with gallons of water. But, during the next twenty-four hours, fresh rubbish and filth are thrown into the drain, and the next morning the lay brothers and the novices again clean it out with gallons of water. This process goes on every day. If the lay brothers and novices were to become discouraged with the fact that fresh filth and rubbish always appeared, and should cease to clean the drain, in a few months the whole monastery would be buried in filth and rubbish." The senior Abbot smiled and said, "I can never argue with the Thingazar. I withdraw my criticism of the King's proposal, and will undertake to assist His Majesty to clean out the drain."

THE BRITISH ENVOY

The High Commissioner of Lower Burma, Sir Arthur Phayre, had arrived at Mandalay as the envoy of Queen Victoria. In the audience chamber of the palace and before the assembled abbots and courtiers, the British Envoy presented to the King various gifts from his sovereign. Among these was a powerful telescope, which the King passed round to the abbots and courtiers to inspect.

After the ceremony of presentation was over, the King and the envoy conversed on many subjects. Sir Arthur Phayre said, "Your Majesty, I have a great respect for the teachings of Buddhism, but I find it difficult to accept the superstitions. For example, I am told the Burmese believe that the Buddha, although six feet tall, appeared sometimes as big as a mountain and at other times as small as a sesame seed. How can that be?" The King turned to the Thingazar Sayadaw and invited him to answer the envoy's question.

"Great Envoy," requested the Thingazar Sayadaw, "will you please look out of the window and tell me how far Mandalay Hill is from this audience hall?" "My lord," Sir Arthur Phayre replied, "it is about three miles." "But some can say that it is only a few yards away," asserted the Sayadaw, "and others can say it is some ten miles away." "My lord," objected Sir Arthur Phayre, "I do not think anyone can misjudge the distance to that extent." The Sayadaw smiled and said, "Great Envoy, if one looks through your telescope from the correct end, the hill will seem only a few yards away, and if one looks through it from the wrong end, the hill will seem to be some ten miles away." Sir Arthur Phayre bowed deeply and said, "My lord has answered my question well."

59. The Great Monk in Despair

CHARMS OF INVULNERABILITY

While residing at Rangoon, the Thingazar Sayadaw overheard some laymen discussing magic and charms. One said that he had known a famous boxer who never bled from any blow because he carried a charm of invulnerability. Another said that he had known a soldier who was never wounded in battle because he had some runes tattooed on his body, which repelled the sword or spear or bullet. The Sayadaw smiled and commented, "Please find me a magician who will make me invulnerable against abuse, prejudice, unfair criticism, and false accusations."

THE THREE GAMBLERS OF RANGOON

One day three fashionably dressed young men came to the Thingazar Sayadaw and challenged him to a disputation about morality. They were obviously a little drunk and the Sayadaw after one glance guessed that they had come straight from the weekly horse races which were becoming so popular in Rangoon. "Laymen," the Sayadaw asked with a weary smile, "I think that you have come from the races. Is it true that bookmakers accept all bets?" "Not all, my lord," replied the young men, "they can reject some bets." "Very good," exclaimed the Sayadaw, "I also can reject any challenge to a disputation. There is no bet and please leave my presence immediately."

THE MOUNTAIN OF GEMS

A young monk said to the Thingazar Sayadaw, "My lord, please accept me as a pupil and let me study at your feet. Teach me to become a wonderful teller of tales." The Sayadaw frowned and replied, "Monk you renounced the world, you entered this Noble Order, and you spent many an hour studying the scriptures. After all that endeavor, you want to become a mere teller of tales. Do you mean to exchange the gold of the scriptures for the dross of my tales? A man, after a weary climb, reaches the peak of the mountain of gems. He sees emeralds and rubies around him, but, losing his interest in them, he searches for a piece of flint for his tinderbox. Oh, Monk, you are as foolish as that man."

A CONVERSATION WITH COLONEL OLCOTT

Colonel H. S. Olcott, the American philanthropist who played a great part in the revival of Buddhism in Ceylon, had been touring Burma, and he said to the Thingazar Sayadaw, "My lord in spite of your great efforts to keep the light of Buddhism burning in Lower Burma, the monks seem to be neglecting the religion. Admittedly, because of your prestige as a monk of great learning and absolute purity, the monks are now well disciplined and well behaved. But they have as a body discarded their role of teachers of religion and morality to the people, and have become mere civil servants in the pay of the British government. Accepting stipends from the new government, they now spend their time teaching elementary mathematics and surveying to their pupils in their monasteries." "Great Layman," replied the Sayadaw, "at the beginning of the rainy season, the farmer plows his large field and, at the same time, in one small corner he makes a nursery of small paddy plants. As the rain continues to fall, he anxiously digs drains round his nursery to keep away the water. In ordinary times he can manage to keep his nursery above water, but, in a year of catastrophic deluge, floods will occur, the young plants in the nursery will die, and after the floods have abated the field will remain barren because no transplanting can take place. Great Layman, I am the farmer, the monasteries are my nurseries, and Lower Burma is my field. I could have dealt with an ordinary deluge of new ideas but not with a catastrophic flood. Alas, as you have noted, my nurseries are now under water and I cannot hope to drain it out."

Tales by
Other Monks

1. How the Pole Star Changed Its Place

Prologue: Two ardent scholars came before the Salin Sayadaw in breathless haste and announced, "My lord, after careful study of the scriptures, we have made a great discovery. We find that Mount Meyyu, on which the gods have their abode, is hollow inside." The Sayadaw smiled and commented, "Laymen, perhaps I must ask you to keep your discovery a secret, as Uncle Golden Simple asked his Nephew."

Uncle Golden Simple considered himself to be very learned, and took great pride in being able to answer the many questions of his precocious Nephew. One evening, as the two sat in front of their house under a clear sky, the Nephew suddenly asked, "Uncle, please show me the Pole Star." Uncle Golden Simple looked up at the sky, and to his chagrin he realized that he did not know the Pole Star. However, determined not to confess his ignorance, he pointed his finger at a star and announced airily, "My boy, yonder is the Pole Star." The Nephew looked, and said with a puzzled frown, "But, Uncle, your star is in the south, whereas the Pole Star must be in the north, as only today my teacher taught me the following lines:

To the north, the Pole Star,
To the south, the Fisher's Net."

There was a pause, during which Uncle Golden Simple collected his thoughts. Then he said, "Nephew, the Pole Star moved to the south only three days ago and the King's astrologers, for reasons of state, have kept it a secret. So I must ask you, my boy, not to give away the secret to your teacher."

2. The Quiet Chicken

Prologue: The Salin Sayadaw was displeased with the poor progress in studies made by a particular group of monks in his monastery. Although young, they were quiet and appeared to be serious and mature, and the Sayadaw had had high hopes that they would in due course, become brilliant scholars. Now, in his disappointment, he said, "My pupils, admittedly you are quiet, you are aloof, you are obedient, and you are not frivolous, and all of you seem to have the makings of a scholar. However, you have not progressed at all in your studies. I hope you will not disappoint me as the Quiet Chicken disappointed his master."

Farmer noticed that among his brood of newly hatched chickens there was one who stayed aloof from the others, who never twittered or screeched, and who did not run around the farmyard. After a few days of careful observation, the Farmer said proudly to his Wife, "Look at my Quiet Chicken. A pot full to the brim with water makes no noise, a soldier with real courage makes no boast, and surely my Quiet Chicken will grow up into a fighting cock and gain great renown for himself and great fortune from bets won for me." The Wife looked at the chicken and disagreed. "Husband, I am sure your chicken is a fool and a coward. Otherwise, he would be strutting about the farmyard with his companions."

The Farmer took special care of his chicken and fed him well until he grew into a big fine bird. But he remained quiet as before and would not mix with the other fowls in the farmyard. Feeling pleased and satisfied, the Farmer took the Quiet Cock to the market place, and, after making heavy bets, placed the bird in the cockpit. The Quiet Cock looked at his adversary in the pit, quietly turned around, and fled.

3. How the Head-Clerk Failed to Keep the Sabbath

Prologue: The Thitseint Sayadaw, after giving the formula of the Eight Precepts to a group of visitors from Lower Burma, smiled and said, "Laymen, I am relieved to find that you are not like the Head-Clerk who failed to keep the Sabbath."

The Head-Clerk in a Lower Burmese town was not a religious man, and he had never been to a monastery. His Wife, however, was very religious. One full-moon day the Wife came back from the monastery and complained, "Husband, all your junior clerks were at the monastery and were asking after you. They made fun of you when I told them that you were at home and they called you an inconsiderate husband when they realized that I had to rush back to the house to give you your morning meal." The Head-Clerk ate his meal in silence and then said, "Wife, I feel very much ashamed that I am the only one from the office who does not keep the Sabbath. However, it is now too late for regrets and, moreover, I do not know how to keep the Sabbath." "Husband, you can keep the Sabbath today," explained the Wife, "because it is still one full hour to noon. As to how to keep the Sabbath, go to the Abbot and repeat what he recites."

The Head-Clerk hastened to the monastery and knelt before the Abbot. The Abbot was pleased to see him and greeted him with the words, "Layman,

I presume that you want the formula of the Eight Precepts from me?" The Head-Clerk, remembering his Wife's instructions, and thinking that it was part of the ritual, repeated exactly the Abbot's question. The Abbot, thinking that the Head-Clerk had come to make fun of the monks and the Sabbath-keepers, said, "You are a foolish man." The Head-Clerk repeated faithfully, "You are a foolish man." At this the Abbot shouted, "Do not disturb the peace of the Sabbath! Leave my monastery at once!" The Head-Clerk shouted back, "Do not disturb the peace of the Sabbath! Leave my monastery at once!" The Abbot now lost his temper and, being stout and strong, he seized hold of the offending Head-Clerk and threw him out of the door. The Head-Clerk went back to his Wife, and with a crestfallen expression said, "I must take some wrestling lessons before I can learn to keep the Sabbath."

4. The Lay Brother Who Was Fond of Eating Corn on the Cob

Prologue: The rains were late, and the worried farmers offered special alms food to the Thitseint Sayadaw and other monks. One of the farmers remarked, "As all the great monks present here are truly pious, rain must fall soon." The Thitseint Sayadaw smiled and said, "We hope the rains will come soon, but, if they do not come, do not put the whole blame on us." Then he proceeded to tell the farmers about the Lay Brother who was fond of eating corn on the cob.

The village monastery was situated at the edge of a cornfield, and the Lay Brother of the monastery was so fond of eating roasted corn on the cob that one night he stole some corn from the field. However, when he roasted and ate the corn, he found it tasteless. He felt that he had been cheated of his rights, and the next morning he went to the farmer and scolded him, "You are a good-for-nothing farmer. Obviously you do not know how to select good seedlings, you do not know how to plant them, and you do not know how to water them. No wonder your corn is so poor." "I did my best," explained the Farmer. "But, Lay Brother, look at the cracks in the ground, and you will see how parched it is."

The Lay Brother walked across the field, and, observing the cracks in the ground, exclaimed, "The Earth Goddess is a good-for-nothing female! She is to be blamed for the poor taste of the corn. The Earth Goddess made herself visible and protested, "Lay Brother, the ground is by nature fertile, but as rainfall has been scanty this year, what can I do?" The Lay Brother paused to consider the matter, and then he agreed that the Earth Goddess was not blameworthy. He looked up into the sky and shouted, "This Rain God is a good-for-nothing fellow! If he had dropped a little more rain on the field, the corn would have been wonderful." The Rain God now made himself visible and explained, "Lay Brother, do you not know that rains fall abundantly in a country only when its king is just and righteous?" The Lay Brother after some thought exonerated the Rain God from blame and went back to the monastery.

For days the Lay Brother brooded over the matter and finally he marched off to the golden city and sought an audience with the King. When he was brought before the King he blurted out, "The fields are parched and cracked, and the corn tastes like wood, because there is a drought. And there is a drought because Your Majesty is not a just and righteous King." "Lay Brother," replied the King, "I am just and righteous, but that is not enough to bring abundant rain. The people themselves have to be just and righteous also. Lay Brother," the King went on, "are you sure that you are just and righteous yourself?" Only then did the Lay Brother realize that, as he was a common thief, he did not deserve to eat good corn.

5. The Scriptures as a Mischief-Maker

Prologue: The Thitseint Sayadaw was invited by a layman to come and honor him by taking alms food at his residence on a certain day. Later on, another layman made a similar request and for the same day. The Sayadaw, forgetting that he was already engaged to go to the first layman's house on that day, accepted the second invitation. When the appointed day came, both laymen arrived at the monastery to escort the Sayadaw to their houses, and only then did the monk realize that he had made a mistake. Turning to the second layman, the Sayadaw apologized. "Worthy layman, I am a forgetful old monk, and I accepted your invitation forgetting that I had already promised to go and receive alms food at the other layman's residence. The scriptures require that I go to the other layman's residence, and the same scriptures forbid me from eating a second breakfast. But do not frown, worthy layman, for I will send a senior monk to go with you as my deputy. Please do not be annoyed with me, and do not blame the scriptures as a mischief-maker."

I n a village there lived a Farmer and his Wife together with their only Son. This Son was very lazy and, although he had long ago finished his education and training at the monastery, he stubbornly refused to help his father in the fields or to find some employment outside. He was also a glutton and so spent his entire time in sleeping or in eating. At last the Farmer, deciding to give a gentle reminder to his Son, said, "My dear Son, while at the monastery you must have learnt the Beatitudes of life, and surely you remember the following lines from the scriptures:

Offering to one's mother and father
Gifts of money and kindIs a blessing of life."

The Son thought for a moment and then replied, "Dear Father, I do remember those wonderful lines, but I also remember the following:

Feeding and clothing of one's children,
Looking after all their needs,
Is a blessing of life."

At this reply the Father lost his temper and a violent quarrel between the Father and Son resulted. Hearing their angry shouts, the Mother came in and made peace between the two antagonists, saying, "Oh, those naughty scriptures! They make mischief between even father and son."

6. The Stall-Holder Who Asked for Time To Say Farewell to His Wife

Prologue: One Sabbath day, after the Khinmagan Sayadaw had given his sermon, a layman from among the audience declared loudly, "I am so tired of life that I want to take a short cut to Nirvana." The Sayadaw smiled and said, "Are you sure that you will not ask for time to say farewell to your wife?"

A Stall-Holder in the Royal Market at Mandalay was a very religious person, and every evening after the day's business he went to a pagoda nearby and spent one full hour telling his beads. At the conclusion of his hour of meditation, he always exclaimed loudly, "For this deed of merit, may I reach Nirvana as speedily as possible!"

A Tradesman from the same market was a mischievous fellow, and he made fun of the religious Stall-Holder every morning. But the Stall-Holder did not waver in his religious pursuits and continued to go to the pagoda every evening. The mischievous Tradesman finally decided to play a trick on him. So he borrowed the costume of a god from a company of strolling players, and, one evening, dressed in the costume, he waited behind a stone pillar at the pagoda. When the Stall-Holder exclaimed as usual, "For this deed of merit, may I reach Nirvana as speedily as possible!" the Tradesman showed himself in the dim light and said, "Worthy Stall-Holder, I am the guardian god of this pagoda and will take you to Nirvana immediately." The Stall-Holder knelt down before the seeming god and expressed his gratitude, but asked for time to go home and say farewell to his wife.

7. The Merchant Who Demanded A Superior Sermon

Prologue: After the Khinmagan Sayadaw had concluded his sermon a layman approached him and said, "The sermon your lordship has just given is an ordinary sermon for ordinary people. But I am a dullard, my lord, and I need an inferior sermon." The Sayadaw smiled and said, "Layman, unlike a merchant with varying qualifies of merchandise, I have only one kind of sermon. Your request, however, shows that you are more humble than the Merchant who asked for a superior sermon."

A Farmer went to a shop and inquired whether a fresh supply of dried fish from Lower Burma had arrived. "It has," replied the Merchant who owned the shop. "How many viss do you require, and do you want the ordinary kind or the superior land?" "Give me a viss of the ordinary kind," requested the Farmer. "I am offering it as alms food to the Lord Abbot in the morning as it is a Sabbath day. I wish I could buy the superior kind but I do not have enough money to do so." The next morning the Farmer fried the dried fish and offered it to the Lord Abbot, who found it tasty. After the meal the Abbot gave a sermon on the merit the Farmer obtained as the result of his good deed in offering such delicious food as alms to a monk. The villagers who were assembled in the monastery for the Sabbath congratulated the Farmer repeatedly, until the Merchant became quite jealous.

When the next Sabbath day came, the Merchant took a viss of superior quality dried fish from his shop, and, after frying it, offered it as alms food to the Abbot. The Abbot again found the fish tasty, and gave a sermon on the merit the Merchant obtained as the result of his good deed in offering such delicious food as alms to a monk. But the Merchant was not satisfied. "My lord," he protested, "today's sermon is exactly similar to the one that was given last Sabbath day. But the dried fish offered by the Farmer was of ordinary quality, whereas the dried fish offered by me today was of superior quality, and surely, my lord, I deserve a superior sermon. The Abbot thought for a while and then replied, "Layman, in that case the merit gained by the Farmer was ordinary merit, whereas the merit gained by you today is superior merit."

8. How a King of Arakan Went Forth to the Royal Park

Prologue: One Sabbath day a middle-aged man came to the Bhamo Sayadaw and asked, "My lord, may I become an inmate of this monastery? I am tired of the world and desire to forsake it. I have made adequate provision for my wife and children and I have their full release." "You are to be praised for renouncing the mundane world," replied the Sayadaw. "I presume that you wish to be ordained a monk as soon as possible." "I do not aspire to be a monk, my lord," the Layman explained. "I do not feel that I can take the 227 vows of a monk." "Then you want to become a novice?" asked the Sayadaw. "I am afraid not," the Layman replied. "Even the Ten Precepts of a novice are beyond me, because I cannot forego my evening meals." The Sayadaw frowned and asked, "Then how will you join my monastery?" "As a lay brother, my lord," answered the Layman. The Sayadaw smiled and said, "Layman, you remind me of how a King of Arakan Went Forth to the Royal Park."

The newly crowned King of Arakan announced to his ministers that he wished to visit the Royal Park, which was some few miles from the golden palace. His ministers inquired, "Will it please Your Majesty to go in the state carriage?" "The jolting of the carriage will give me a nasty headache," replied the King. "Then, will it please Your Majesty to ride on the white elephant?" asked the ministers. "The elephant's back is too high," the King explained, "and heights always make me dizzy." "We presume then that Your Majesty will ride the white charger," the ministers opined. "Oh, not at all," answered the King. "That horse goes too fast and I will become sick." The ministers were puzzled and one of them was bold enough to ask, "Then, how will Your Majesty go forth to the royal park?" "Bring me a goat, ordered the King, "I will ride him to the park."

9. The Puppet Showman Who Overslept

Prologue: The quiet of the monastery was suddenly broken by a newly ordained middle-aged monk, who was abusing and shouting at the small boys whom he was teaching. The Bhamo Sayadaw at once sent for the angry monk and asked him why he was using such angry and abusive language. "I am very sorry, my lord," apologized the monk. "But, as your lordship is aware, until last lent I was a master carpenter, who had been used to shouting and to abusing his young apprentices." "But this is a monastery," the Sayadaw scolded, "and the boys are members of this monastic community." "I realize my fault, my lord," answered the monk with a dejected look, "but I forgot for a moment that I am now a monk." "You wear the robes of a gentle monk," the Sayadaw remarked, "and when abusive and angry words come out of your mouth you become a figure of fun. Listen to this tale of the Puppet Showman who overslept."

Once there lived a Puppet Showman who was loved and respected by everyone all over the countryside for his declamations. His orations always fitted the character of the particular puppet he was manipulating, no matter whether it was the gentle King of the gods or the violent Ogre. However, as his reputation grew he became lazy, and took to sleeping between scenes during shows.

One night he overslept, and, when his frantic assistant woke him up, he brushed him aside with the words, "You fool, am I not the Master Showman? Of course, I know it is now my cue." Seizing hold of the king-god puppet, he raised it over the curtain onto the stage. Poor Master Showman, sleepy Master Showman, he thought he was holding the ogre puppet. So he manipulated the puppet to make it give the ogre dance, and he declaimed with a fierce voice, "I am the ten-headed ogre, and I am fond of human flesh." The audience, seeing the king-god dancing and speaking like an ogre, broke into mocking laughter and thus overnight the Puppet Showman lost his reputation and became a laughing stock.

10. The Widow and the Thief

Prologue: The Payagyi Sayadaw was giving a lecture to his class of young monks and noticed that some of them were yawning and falling asleep. The Sayadaw paused and said, "As some of you are yawning and dozing, I will stop my lesson now, but, as the Old Widow complained aloud for the Thief to overhear, I want to complain, 'Isn't it too early for nocturnal pursuits?' "

An Old Widow lived by herself in a small cottage on the outskirts of her village. One afternoon she sold her harvest of paddy on the field itself, and, as it was still an hour from sundown, she walked back to her cottage at a leisurely pace. Unknown to her, a Thief from a nearby village had been watching her the whole day from a distance. The Thief thought to himself: "She is a careful old woman, and she is certain to close the doors and windows of her cottage once she gets home, so that it would be very difficult for me to get in. If I hurry to the cottage now ahead of her, I can surely get inside through a window. Then I will hide myself in a dark nook or corner and wait till she falls asleep." According to his plan, he walked rapidly past her, and, on reaching her cottage, he climbed through a window and from a hiding place patiently awaited the Widow's arrival. The Widow arrived some moments later and carefully closed the door. Then she looked around and spied the Thief hiding in the corner. However she pretended not to have noticed him because, if she should confront him, the Thief out of sheer desperation would take her money at knife-point.

The Widow sang a gay tune to herself and walked slowly to the front window. Putting her head out, she shouted to her Neighbor, "Gossip, how are you today? What curry are you cooking?" "I am very well, thank you, and I am cooking some chicken," the Neighbor replied. "By the way, Gossip," the old Widow continued, "What is the proper time for thieves to prowl?" "About the hour of midnight and never before the cocks have crowed the second watch," the Neighbor explained. "The sun has not even set," the Widow complained. "Isn't it too early for nocturnal pursuits?" The Thief, overhearing her remarks, jumped out of the back window and ran away.

11. The Son-in-Law Who Set Fire to His Own Beard

Prologue: A novice who had been in the order for two or three years sought permission from the Payagyi Sayadaw to leave the monastic life. "My lord," the novice explained, "I cannot bear to see my parents living in poverty and want, and I feel that I must obtain some suitable employment so as to be able to support them." "Your idea is a noble one," answered the Sayadaw. "But a fine idea is often difficult to translate into reality. You have been an inmate of this monastery since the age of six and a novice since the age of sixteen. You are now too old to take up any craft as an apprentice. Your considerable learning in the scriptures will be of no great use to a layman in these changing times. So, my pupil, I advise you to continue with your religious studies and then take the higher ordination in course of time." The novice, however, refused to change his mind and the same afternoon he left the order.

After some four or five years the former novice visited the monastery with a long tale of woe. He told the Sayadaw of his many troubles. As he could not find regular employment he became an added burden to his parents. Then he fell in love with a girl from the neighborhood and married her, and now the poor parents had to support him, his wife, and two children. "I never realized, my lord," he wept, "that I was an utter fool." The Sayadaw smiled and said, "I feel very sorry for you, but you remind me of the Son-In-Law Who Set Fire to His Own Beard."

The only Daughter of a Farmer fell in love with a young Merchant who was quite rich. But the Farmer objected to the proposed marriage because the young man was too ugly, with a big head and a long beard. However, as the Daughter wept and wailed, and also because of the intercession of his Wife, the Farmer reluctantly gave his consent. The marriage proved to be happy for the young couple, but the Farmer sickened at the sight of his ugly Son-in-Law every morning at breakfast. He complained to his Wife who only scolded him for his prejudice. After some weeks he felt that he could not bear it anymore, and wrote on the wall of the house with a piece of charcoal the following lines:

"Big Head,
Long Beard,
Foolish Mind."

The Son-in-Law read the lines and felt greatly insulted and shamed. "I know I have a big head, and I know I have a long beard, he complained to the Daughter, "but your Father has no right to call me 'foolish', because I am good at my trade." As the Daughter made no comment, the Son-in-Law became very angry with the whole family and with himself. "This wretched beard is the main cause of my misery!" he shouted, and at once set fire to his beard, with the result that not only his beard but his whole face was burnt. As he writhed in pain and the Daughter poured soothing oil on the burns, he moaned, "Your Father was right. I do have a foolish mind."

12. The Village Wiseman and the Elephant Tracks

Prologue: A group of laymen posed this question to the Payagyi Sayadaw: "In Lower Burma, my lord, some butchers and fishermen have become very rich. Are their riches due to merit or demerit from their past existences?" The Sayadaw answered, "Their way of earning a living is not a good way, because it involves the slaughter of many animals, and for this they will have to suffer in their future existences. Nonetheless, they are now rich and live in luxury and comfort because of some good deeds in the past." But the lay preacher in the group, who prided himself on a knowledge of the scriptures, refused to accept the Sayadaw's explanation, and, misquoting and misinterpreting some texts, he argued at length that the butchers' and fishermen's riches were the result of some evil deeds in their past lives. The Sayadaw, after refuting him, smiled and said, "Lay preacher, you remind me of the Village Wiseman and the elephant tracks."

The inhabitants of a small village in Upper Burma were ignorant and foolish, but there was one who was less ignorant but more foolish than the others. The villagers, however, regarded him as their Wiseman and consulted him on all matters that puzzled them from time to time.

One night a rogue elephant wandered into a sugar-cane field belonging to a villager and ate up all the sugar cane. The following morning the owner of the field discovered the loss and was mystified to see the elephant's tracks. It never entered his mind that the tracks were those of an elephant. So he went and fetched the Village Wiseman. The Village Wiseman looked carefully at the elephant tracks and sat down and pondered the whole day. Just as the sun was setting he stood up and announced with a smile, "I have solved the mystery. There are two problems to be considered. First, how could anyone steal the sugar cane without leaving any footprints? Second, what are those large round marks on the ground? The explanation is this: the thief tied a winnowing tray to each foot, came walking across the field, and carried away the sugar cane on his shoulders."

Appendix One

Chronological Table of Burmese Buddhism

	Political Events	Ecclesiastical Events	Events outside Burma
563 B.C.			Birth of Prince Siddhattha Gotama, in India.
528 BC.		According to tradition (1) Shwedagon Pagoda was built during Buddha's lifetime, and	He became the Buddha.
483 B.C.		(2) Arahat Gavampati, a contemporary disciple of the Buddha, brought Buddhism to the Mons.	Death of the Buddha.
482 B.C.			First Great Synod of Monks, in India.
382 B.C.			Second Great Synod of Monks, in India.
3rd Century B.C.	The Pyus (proto-Burmese) in Upper Burma. The Mons in Lower Burma. Mon Kingdom of Thaton.		
253 B.C.			Third Great Synod of Monks, in India, under patronage of Emperor Asoka.

	Political Events	Ecclesiastical Events	Events outside Burma
247 B.C.		Buddhism became the official religion of Thaton.	Asoka's Missions to Thaton, Ceylon, and other parts of Asia.
1st Century B.C.	Pyu Kingdom of Prome in Lower Burma.	Buddhism flourished in the Kingdom.	Break-up of Buddhism into two schools, Theravada and Mahayana. Fourth Great Synod of Monks, in Ceylon.
6th Century A.D.	Decline of Pyu power. Pyus withdrew into Upper Burma. The Burmese entered Upper Burma from the north and fused with the Pyus. Mons supreme in Lower Burma.	Mahayana Buddhism introduced into Upper Burma. Ari monks and "decadent" Buddhism.	
1044	Anawrahta united Burma into a single Kingdom and founded the First Burmese Empire comprising the whole of Indo-China. Fall of Thaton.	Shin Arahan, Mon monk, converted Anawrahta. Ari monks suppressed. Theravada Buddhism became official religion. Shin Arahan appointed primate for the whole Empire. Burma became the main center of Theravada Buddhism.	Muslim Conquest of India. Disappearance of Buddhism from India. Decay of Buddhism in Ceylon. Anawrahta sent mission to Ceylon at the request of its king to re-ordain Sinhalese monks.

	Political Events	Ecclesiastical Events	Events outside Burma
1181		New sect known as Ceylon sect founded by a Mon monk ordained in Ceylon. The Ceylon sect itself split into three sects.	
Circa 1200		Controversy between Forest-Dwelling monks and Town-Village-Dwelling monks.	
1287	Fall of Pagan to Kublai Khan's Tatar armies. Petty Kingdoms all over Burma.	Indiscipline in the ranks of the clergy.	
1364	Emergence of Ava in Upper Burma as the Burmese Kingdom, and Pegu in Lower Burma as the Mon Kingdom.	Primate at Ava. Primate at Pegu.	
1460	Dhammazedi, king of Pegu.		
1475		Royal mission of abbots to Ceylon to seek re-ordination. The king invited monks from Lower Burma, Upper Burma, and othe Kingdoms of Indo-China to take fresh ordination at the capital of Pegu. Reemergence of a single unified sect all over Burma. Primate at Ava and primate at Pegu, but close cooperation between the two.	

	Political Events	Ecclesiastical Events	Events outside Burma
1551	Bayinnaung reunified Burma and founded the Second Burmese Empire, comprising the whole of Indo-China.	Primate for the whole empire.	
1581	Bayinnaung died and his empire disintegrated, but Burma remained united as a single kingdom.	Primate for the whole kingdom.	
1700		Controversy over the proper manner of wearing robes. The orthodox sect insisted that the outer robe must cover both shoulders in a formal manner when outside the monastery. The reform sect argued that the less formal mode of wearing the robe across one shoulder only, was to be preferred, as it would ensure ease of movement and comfort to the monk, without any loss of dignity. Controversy started in Upper Burma but spread to Lower Burma.	
1740	Mons rebelled and restored their monarchy. They conquered Upper Burma.		

	Political Events	Ecclesiastical Events	Events outside Burma
1752	Rebellion of Alaungpaya. He conquered the whole country and founded the Third Burmese Empire.	Primate for the whole empire. As he belonged to the reform sect, the orthodox sect lost ground, but was not persecuted.	
1781	King Bodawpaya. He centralized the government and exercised strong control over the Empire.	(1) Bodawpaya by proclamation decided in favor of the orthodox sect. As a primate lost office with the death of the king who appointed him, Alaungpaya's primate was now an ordinary abbot; he and his more militant supporters were unfrocked by royal decree. (2) Bodawpaya appointed The Thudhamma Ecclesiastical Council of Eight Members and gave it supreme power of control over the whole clergy. Reemergence of a single unified sect, the Thudhamma sect. Bodawpaya, finding that the council was unable to function effectively without a president, appointed one of the eight to be the primate. Thus the power of control over the clergy came to be vested in primate-in-council. (3) Bodawpaya had a doctrinal difference with the primate and wanted to remove him from office, but did not dare to do so. He asked the primate to resign, but the latter refused. Finally, tired with controversy, the primate left the order and became a layman again. A new primate was appointed by Bodawpaya.	

	Political Events	Ecclesiastical Events	Events outside Burma
1815			Whole of Ceylon conquered by the British.
1824–26	First Anglo-Burmese War. Loss of the Indian provinces of Manipur and Assam, and the Burmese maritime provinces of Arakan and Tenasserim, to the British.	Monks in the ceded territory still held themselves responsible to the primate at the Burmese capital.	
1852	Second Anglo-Burmese War and loss of Pegu to the British. Entire Lower Burma now under the British. Mindon leading the peace party at the court, was declared king in place of his brother, Pagan Min.	Monks from Lower Burma migrated to Upper Burma.	
1855–65		(1) The British denied patronage to Buddhism in Lower Burma. (2) King Mindon and his great monks took measures to enforce discipline within the ranks of the clergy in Upper Burma, and encouraged monks to return to Lower Burma.	

	Political Events	Ecclesiastical Events	Events outside Burma
		(3) Okpo Sayadaw in Lower Burma questioned the authority of the primate over monks in Lower Burma, resulting in the emergence of a new sect, the Okpo or Dwarya sect. (4) Criticism of King Mindon and the Ecclesiastical Council by two of his great monks. (5) Shwegyin Sayadaw founded a new sect in Upper Burma.	
1871		Fifth Great Synod of Monks, held by King Mindon. Authority of Ecclesiastical Council again accepted by many monks in Lower Burma, but the Okpo Sayadaw and his followers remained independent. In Upper Burma itself, the Shwegyin sect, while accepting the authority of the Ecclesiastical Council, continued to remain separate.	

	Political Events	Ecclesiastical Events	Events outside Burma
1876	Final humiliation of King Mindon by the British. The fall of the kingdom to the British became inevitable.		
1878	Death of King Mindon and accession of King Theebaw.	The Monk's Tales.	
1885	Third Anglo-Burmese War. All of Burma proclaimed part of the British Empire.		
1948	Burma regained her dependence and seceded from the British Empire.		
1956		Sixth Great Synod of Monks, held at Rangoon.	

Appendix Two

Buddhist Precepts or Rules of Training

I. For the Layman

THE FIVE PRECEPTS

1. To refrain from depriving any living thing of its life.
2. To refrain from taking possession of any article without the permission of its owner.
3. To refrain from illicit sexual relations.
4. To refrain from speaking (or acting) untruthfully.
5. To refrain from taking liquors and drugs, or other intoxicants which engender forgetfulness or slothfulness.

THE EIGHT PRECEPTS

In the Eight Precepts are included the above Five Precepts with the precept against sexual immorality extended thus: To refrain from all sexual relations.

6. To refrain from taking food or other nourishment after the hour of noon.
7. (a) To refrain from singing, dancing, playing on musical instruments, acrobatics, and play-acting (or watching or making others perform).
   (b) To refrain from beautifying the body or the face with flowers, powder, paint, unguents, or ornaments, and to refrain from the use of perfumes and scents.
8. To refrain from sleeping on a high or ornate bed.

THE TEN PRECEPTS

In the Ten Precepts, 7 (a) and 7 (b) above are numbered separately as 7 and 8, and the precept regarding sleeping on a high or ornate bed becomes 9.

10. To refrain from handling (or taking delight in) gold and silver or other currency.

II. For the Novice

THE TEN RULES INVOLVING LOSS OF STATUS AND EXPULSION

1 to 5. The same as 1 to 5 of the Eight and Ten Precepts.
6. To refrain from speaking disrespectfully of the Buddha.
7. To refrain from speaking disrespectfully of His Teachings.
8. To refrain from speaking disrespectfully of the Order.
9. To refrain from holding false beliefs.
10. To refrain from spoiling the character or the personality of a nun.

THE TEN RULES INVOLVING PUNISHMENT

1 to 5. The same as 6 to 10 of the Ten Precepts.
6. To refrain from attempting to stop the offering of alms food and robes to monks.
7. To refrain from attempting to stop the donation of a monastery.
8. To refrain from attempting to cause some disadvantage to monks.
9. To refrain from abusing or slandering monks.
10. To refrain from causing mischief, misunderstanding, or discord among monks.

75 rules of decorum, pertaining to proper demeanor, including proper mode of wearing robes and taking food

III. For the Monk

4 rules involving loss of status and expulsion
1. To refrain from all sexual relations.
2. To refrain from taking possession of any article without the permission of its owner.
3. To refrain from depriving a human being of his or her life.
4. To refrain from boasting of possessing supernormal powers.

13 rules involving trial before an assembly of monks
1. To refrain from causing semen to be emitted.
2. To refrain from wantonly coming into physical contact with a woman.
3. To refrain from speaking lewd or suggestive words to a woman.
4. To refrain from persuading or intimidating a woman with a view to obtaining sexual gratification from her.
5. To refrain from acting as a go-between for a man and a woman.

6. To refrain from constructing a monastery unless it is no larger than 40 feet by 25 feet and is on a suitable site.

7. To refrain from approving the site for a monastery (larger than 40 feet by 25 feet) which a donor offers to build, without the prior inspection, advice, and approval of other monks.

8. To refrain from maliciously bringing a false charge against another monk so that he loses his status and is expelled from the Order.

9. To refrain from maliciously bringing a false charge against another monk under a cloak of legality so that he loses his status and is expelled from the Order.

10. To refrain from causing a schism among monks.

11. To refrain from supporting a monk who is causing a schism among monks.

12. To refrain from answering back or disputing disrespectfully, when reprimanded by other monks for a breach of discipline.

13. To refrain from destroying the regard and respect of the laity for the Order by giving presents of flowers, fruits, bamboo, sand, or soap to laymen or laywomen, or by running errands for them, or by giving medical or magical prescriptions, or by making astrological predictions for them.

2 rules involving either expulsion, trial before an assembly, or mere expiation depending on the evidence and assessment of the guilt by a reliable laywoman

1. To refrain from being alone with a woman in a secluded place. (The reliable laywoman will assess whether sexual intercourse has taken place under Rule 1 of the 4 Rules of Expulsion, or whether the monk has wantonly come into physical contact with the woman under Rule 2 of the 13 Rules above.)

2. To refrain from being alone with a woman at a place where they can be seen but cannot be overheard. (The reliable laywoman will assess whether the monk has spoken lewd or suggestive words under Rule 3 of the 13 Rules above.)

30 rules involving forfeiture and expiation

These rules relate to the acquisition of prohibited articles and the improper acquisition of articles permissible for monks to possess, as, for example:

1. To refrain from possessing more than three robes.

5. To refrain from accepting a robe from a nun who is not a relation except in exchange.

9. To refrain from hinting to two or more donors that they should pool their resources and offer a more expensive robe.

18. To refrain from accepting gold or silver.
21. To refrain from possessing a second begging bowl for more than ten days.
30. To refrain from appropriating any article which is the common property of the monks.

92 rules involving expiation
The following are examples:

1. To refrain from speaking (or acting) untruthfully.
2. To refrain from using insulting words.
3. To refrain from uttering slander.
10. To refrain from digging the ground.
11. To refrain from destroying vegetation.
21. To refrain from instructing nuns unless specially appointed to do so.
33. To refrain from accepting invitations to meals except in strict order of priority of time.
35. To refrain from partaking of more food after finishing a meal.
37. To refrain from partaking of food after noon.
44. To refrain from being alone with a woman in a secluded place.
45. To refrain from being alone with a woman at a place where they can be seen but cannot be overheard.
48. To refrain from visiting an army that is on active service.
51. To refrain from taking liquors and drugs or other intoxicants which engender forgetfulness or slothfulness.
61. To refrain from depriving any living thing of its life.
74. To refrain from striking another monk in anger.
87. To refrain from having in his cell a couch or chair which is higher or longer than the prescribed height and length.
88. To refrain from having in his cell a couch or a chair which is padded with cotton or similar material.

4 rules involving mere confession

1. To refrain from accepting food from a nun.
2. To refrain from allowing a nun to supervise the serving of alms food.
3. To refrain from begging for alms from families which are in straitened circumstances, except by their special prior invitation.
4. To refrain from permitting lay-men and laywomen to bring alms food without prior notice while residing in a forest or such unsafe place. (When prior notice is given, the monk will be able to warn them of wild animals, bandits, and other possible harms on the way.)

Appendix Three

After the Time of the Thingazar Sayadaw

Although the Thingazar Sayadaw strove to the very end of his life to lift Burmese Buddhism above the tumult of nationalism and politics so that it could continue to flourish under an alien government, his remarks to Colonel Olcott in 1885 clearly showed that he was distressed and disappointed with the apparent lack of results. His contemporaries also thought that he had failed because, soon after his death, the Nget-twin Sayadaw, now settled in the small town of Twante, a few miles from Rangoon, permitted his followers to declare that a new sect had been founded with the name of the Nget-twin sect, while the Junior Chapter continued to grow in size and popularity. In addition, a few monks even joined the guerrillas who fought so desperately against the British for some four years after the annexation of the kingdom; like any other guerrilla, they were captured, handcuffed, flogged, shot, or hanged still wearing their yellow robes. As time passed, however, it became obvious to all that, had it not been for the labors of the Thingazar Sayadaw, there would have been many more sects and many more monks involved in the hopeless battle against the new rulers. When the period of transition passed, and British rule was firmly established over the country, it was found that Buddhism and the Burmese way of life had survived the great national catastrophe of loss of independence and that the Buddhist faith and the Buddhist clergy had continued to flourish although deprived of royal patronage under foreign rule. In the renewed struggle against British rule in the period 1910–39, the Burmese found it impossible to keep their national aspirations and their national religion distinct and apart, but they did try to remember the lessons taught by the Thingazar Sayadaw in his sermons and in his tales.

The first national movement for freedom after the suppression of the guerrillas was in the formation of Buddhist societies and Buddhist schools in the period 1910–20. During that decade no open nationwide challenge to British authority was ever made, and the Buddhist schools, following the pattern set by the Christian mission schools, accepted financial aid from the government and conformed to its curriculum. In 1920, however, the students of the newly established Rangoon University staged a strike in protest against the dominance of the university by British professors and the government, and their action was approved and endorsed by the students in schools—

state, missionary, and Buddhist—all over the country. The government at first took stern measures and declared all striking students expelled, but, in the face of widespread sympathy and support extended to the students by the nation as a whole, the government had to compromise by amending the university act and canceling its declaration of expulsion. Although the strike was called off by the students, it was followed by a boycott of British goods. A religious undertone was given to the strike and the boycott by the use of the Burmese term "to turn the begging bowl upside down" to describe both actions. This term related to the seldom exercised right of Burmese Buddhist monks to show their displeasure with a wayward layman by refusing to accept alms food offered by him. Such an action did not, of course, amount to an excommunication of the layman, because Buddhism was never organized into a church, and a person became a Buddhist by merely professing the religion, without the necessity of going through a ceremony of baptism or similar ritual of admission. It did, however, result in social ostracism. Further religious flavor was added by the fact that the students during the strike repaired to nearby monasteries to attend the "parallel" classes held there by volunteer teachers, and were looked after and fed by the resident monks. During the boycott of British goods some fiery young monks at Mandalay and Rangoon roamed the markets, admonishing those who were wearing or buying clothes of British manufacture.

The nationalist leaders became alarmed lest their religion should become tainted with politics, and hastened to take suitable measures to prevent such an eventuality. Thus, when the patriotic Buddhist associations were amalgamated into one supreme national body, the new organization was named the General Council of Burmese Associations, rather than General Council of Buddhist Associations. The Buddhist schools were also renamed national schools. Although a few monks, as, for example, Sayadaw U Ottama and Sayadaw U Wizara, did emerge as political leaders, abbots and most laymen openly deplored the participation of monks in politics. In the final struggles for freedom during the period 1939–48, the monks gradually moved away from politics, and when independence finally came in 1948, and the new constitution was promulgated, both the laity and the clergy warmly applauded the legislature for its decision that, in conformity with ancient tradition and established custom, Burmese Buddhist monks should remain without any franchise. The same constitution restored state patronage to Buddhism, without making it the state religion, and the new Burmese government immediately started preparations to hold the Sixth Great Synod of Buddhism in 1956 on the twenty-five-hundredth anniversary of the Buddha's passing away.

Bibliography

Books in English

Conze, Edward. Buddhism. Oxford, Bruno Cassirer, 1951.

Cowell, E. B. *The Jataka*. 6 vols. Cambridge University Press, 1905.

Dutt, Nalinaksha. *Early Monastic Buddhism*. Calcutta, Oriental Book Agency. 1960.

Horner, I. B. *The Vinaya*. 6 vols. London, Pali Text Society, 1958.

Htin Aung, Maung. *Burmese Drama*. Oxford University Press, 1937.

———. *Burmese Folk-Tales*. Oxford University Press, 1948.

———. *Burmese Law Tales*. Oxford University Press, 1962.

———. *Folk Elements in Burmese Buddhism*. Oxford University Press, 1962.

———. *The Stricken Peacock: An Account of Anglo-Burmese Relations 1752–1948*. The Hague, Nijhoff, 1955.

Humphreys, Christmas. *Buddhism*, London, Penguin Books, 1951.

Law, B. C. *Sasanavamsa: A History of Buddhism in Burma*. Sacred Books of the East Vol. XVII. Luzac, London, 1952.

Slater, R. H. *Paradox and Nirvana*. Chicago University Press, 1951.

Thomas, Edward J. *The Life of Buddha*. London, Kegan Paul, 1956.

Trager, Helen. *Burma Through Alien Eyes*. Bombay, Asia Publishing House, 1965.

Wapola-Rahula. *What the Buddha Taught*. London, Gordon Fraser, 1959.

Books in Burmese

Hmannan Yazawin (The glass palace chronicle of the kings of Burma). 5 Vols. Mandalay, Upper Burma Press, 1908. (Vol. I translated into English by Pe Maung Tin and G. H. Luce. Burma Research Society, 1923.)

Konbaungzet Mahayazawin (The chronicle of the Alaungpaya dynasty), edited by Pagan U Tin. Rangoon, Thudhammawaddi Press, 1922. The editor was a junior minister under King Theebaw.

Sasanalankara (A history of Buddhism in Burma), by Maha Dhamma Thingyan. Rangoon, Hanthawaddi Press, 1956. The author was a minister under King Mindon.

Sasana-bahussuttappakasani (Notes on the history of Buddhism in Burma), by U Yazinda. Rangoon, Hanthawaddi Press, 1953. U Yazinda wrote this volume in 1928.

Shwegaingthar. *Mandalay*. Mandalay, Kyeepwayay Press, 1960.

Thingazar Sagabon Paunggyoke (The collected epigrams of the Thingazar Sayadaw), printed and published by Saya Thein at Rangoon, 1911.

Tracts issued from time to time by the Ngettwin Monastery, Twante (near Rangoon) and by the Okpo-Dwarya Sect.

ABOUT PARIYATTI

Pariyatti is dedicated to providing affordable access to authentic teachings of the Buddha about the Dhamma theory (*pariyatti*) and practice (*paṭipatti*) of Vipassana meditation. A 501(c)(3) nonprofit charitable organization since 2002, Pariyatti is sustained by contributions from individuals who appreciate and want to share the incalculable value of the Dhamma teachings. We invite you to visit www.pariyatti.org to learn about our programs, services, and ways to support publishing and other undertakings.

Pariyatti Publishing Imprints

Vipassana Research Publications (focus on Vipassana as taught by S.N. Goenka in the tradition of Sayagyi U Ba Khin)

BPS Pariyatti Editions (selected titles from the Buddhist Publication Society, copublished by Pariyatti in the Americas)

Pariyatti Digital Editions (audio and video titles, including discourses)

Pariyatti Press (classic titles returned to print and inspirational writing by contemporary authors)

Pariyatti enriches the world by

- disseminating the words of the Buddha,
- providing sustenance for the seeker's journey,
- illuminating the meditator's path.